CODE:
POLONAISE

CODE:
POLONAISE

by EVA-LIS WUORIO

HOLT, RINEHART AND WINSTON

NEW YORK   CHICAGO   SAN FRANCISCO

BOOKS BY EVA-LIS WUORIO

Code: Polonaise
Save Alice!
Venture At Midsummer
October Treasure

For my god-daughter Sarah
who was not born
when *these* children were in peril.

To help her think of other lands and people
with understanding.

This motto is traditionally displayed
on the banners of the Polish Legion:

Think, think of us, O Poland of mine
when we shall be already gone!
Have we not made of your name a prayer
that weeps and a thunder that lightens?

Prologue

I don't know if you have ever thought about it, but there have been children in all the stories told, as long as our recorded history exists.

There were stories about children drawn on stone 5,000 years before Christ was born, discovered when the earliest settlements of Egypt and Mesopotamia were found by archeologists.

That's about 7,000 years by our counting.

About 3,500 years ago, before our Christian civilization by which we count time, there were stories about children—in inscriptions—from the Sumerian civilization.

Three thousand years before Christ, which

1

makes it nearly 5,000 by our counting, the Egyptians were recording the things their children did, in hieratic writing. That was during the first Egyptian Dynasty. There were also pictorial writings in the Minoan Age in Crete.

It's nearly 2,000 years since our Christian calendar began. In the many centuries since, children have been just as important as young people and adults in the histories of their countries.

They have been sung about in folk songs; they figure in the Viking sagas; they do brave deeds in the ancient legends. You'll always find children in a good story. Why not? If there were no children there would be no grownups. Quite often they can help a lot.

In our own times, we have lots of stories about children too. We read about happy times and happy families, happy adventures, happy years.

But if you think of it, the children are there in tragic times as well.

In the past few years, there have been the children of Hungary and Czechoslovakia, of Korea and Vietnam, of Biafra and other South African countries, who have faced danger, and fear, and hunger. And there are children who have faced great personal sadness in America as well.

This story begins two years after 1939 when Hitler and his Nazi German Army occupied Poland. It is a story about Jan and Wanda, Stas and Pawel, and the rest of them. Just children. They

2

may not be actually real people, but there were many who were just like them—some are still alive. Everything they did and everything that happened to them is real, and true.

One shadow in the dark archway moved. Then tramping steps echoed out in the old square. They rang loud and sharp in the narrow lane. The shadow was still. Even the old houses seemed to hold their breath.

Moonlight threw into silhouette a soldier in the square German helmet, rifle at the ready, marching into the lane. He and his companions threw huge, menacing shadows that followed them like another ghostly patrol.

The thin boy in the archway melted into the darkness of ruins behind him. Careful as he was, his feet released a dribble of loose stones.

The Germans stopped. In defeated Warsaw, even a sound of loose rubble could spell danger. The Poles were fools. They didn't know when they were defeated. It was better to be careful.

But there was no sound now, and after a moment, they tramped on.

The boy waited. Then he dashed out into the square. There was still one house, one doorway, left intact. Swiftly he unrolled a piece of paper, smeared it with potato glue and slapped it on the door.

He began to whistle as he made sure the paper stuck to the door.

The thunder of the German patrol's boots came back in a rush. The boy stood, frozen by his own carelessness.

Right then the next phrase of the well-known tune rang out:

"Here!" The voice was right behind him. "Quick!"

The boy made a leap into the rubbled

house. Someone caught him and pushed him down. He lay still.

When the Germans came running out of the lane into the square, it was empty but for the moonlight and the ruins.

The officer of the guard pushed back his helmet and scratched his head.

"You heard it, didn't you?" he shouted at his patrol.

"Like a whistle," one of the men said. "Like a wind, maybe, in all these rotten rocks."

"These stupid Poles have nothing to whistle about."

The moon passed behind a cloud and they did not see the notice the boy had pasted on the door. They marched on, stamping their feet as they had been taught to do.

Behind the crumbling wall of a bombed house two shadows moved again. The boy felt his hand taken into a thin hand. Stumbling, he followed his unseen guide through stone and rubble and broken steps. Then there were steps going down.

"Lift this." The words were a whisper.

He could tell it was the catch of a trap door. It was heavy, but it came up easily as though it was in constant use. He felt steps leading down. When he lowered the trap above him, there was no longer any wind.

"You are certainly a bright one to whistle

6

Chopin outside the Gestapo quarters," a voice said clearly out of the darkness.

"I was an idiot," the boy admitted. "Who are you?"

"Wait. I'm trying to light a candle."

A tallow candle sputtered into a dim flame. They moved into its light.

"Wanda!"

"Jan Kolenko!"

The two children stared at one another in utter amazement. The girl's shoulder length, thick, fair hair framed her face. Her gray eyes were wide-spaced. Jan Kolenko was a head taller—a thin, dark boy with a forelock of black hair and a stubborn mouth.

"That's the piece you were rehearsing for our last school concert." Wanda broke the silence. "The thing you whistled. Chopin's 'Polonaise Militaire.' "

"Yes. I can't get the music out of my mind. But it was bad discipline, whistling out there. How stupid can I get! If you report me to the underground, they'll probably throw me out."

"I won't. I don't know anyone in the underground anyhow."

"What are you doing here?" Jan was trying to see into the blackness beyond the candlelight.

"I'm living here." The girl tried to speak matter-of-factly. "First, after the invasion I lived with my Aunt Flika, but she died. Then the Rodozkis looked after me. Remember? He was our history teacher. Five days ago, he had to leave suddenly—the Gestapo were after him. His wife went with him. Of course they couldn't take me."

"But your own people?"

"Mother was killed in one of the first bombings. Papa was with the army. I don't know where he is now—he never came back."

"It's a queer thing," Jan said slowly, "I've been an orphan since I was a little boy, and I used to be sorry for myself. Now, I sometimes feel sorry for others. I hadn't so much to lose."

Suddenly, he cupped his hands around the candle flame. "What's that?"

There had been a whimpering, snuffling sound in the darkness.

Now a baby's voice quavered, "Mummy? Wanda?"

Wanda picked up the candle. Jan followed her to the corner of the cellar. There, in a wooden packing case half-filled with newspapers, wrapped in a worn blanket, was a little boy. He couldn't be quite three yet. He looked very small.

His face was flushed with sleep. He blinked and pointed a stubby finger at Jan. "Who are you?" he said.

"Who is *he?*" Jan said.

"Pawel. I found him."

"*Found him!*"

"Yes. Three days ago. He was sitting by himself out there on the square. I asked everybody who's still living or hiding in the ruins around here,

8

and down the lanes. No one knew him. I couldn't just leave him, could I? Nobody wanted him."

"Had a bad dweam," Pawel told them.

"It's all right now, Wanda's here." She wrapped him up again and gave him a kiss. "What am I going to do with him?"

"Tomorrow we'll look for his parents," Jan said.

"The only thing *he* can tell me is that his name is Pawel," Wanda explained.

"We'll figure out something. Look, Wanda, I've spoiled this place for you. When they find the sign I put up practically next door to you, they'll rout out the neighborhood."

"Yes," Wanda said. Her eyes stared up at Jan, huge. "Yes."

"I tell you what. I'm living in a deserted house with Stas. Remember Stas Rowski who took music with us? Well, it isn't a bad place. You and Pawel had better come there. Get your things."

In the candlelight, unexpectedly, Wanda grinned. "What things? I've just got Pawel, two blankets, a crust of bread, and three potatoes I was saving for tomorrow."

As they got Wanda's few belongings together, Jan said, "Did you hear the German radio car today? That's why Stas and I are out tonight, putting up signs. The Nazis had a loudspeaker screaming, 'Poland Is Dead. Poland Will Never Rise Again.'"

Jan picked up soundly sleeping Pawel and started up the cellar steps.

"What did your signs say?"

Jan said:

"POLAND STILL LIVES"

2

The moon had come out by the time Wanda, Jan, and Pawel finally reached the house where the two boys lived on the outskirts of Warsaw.

It was a one-story house with four high pillars supporting a porch. It looked lopsided because the entire right wing was in ruins. The plaster had seemed white only because of the moonlight. Overgrown bushes hid the broken windows.

"Our mansion," Jan said. "It's wiser not to try to repair anything outside. The more of a ruin it looks the less likely the Nazis are to take an interest in us."

He led the way around the house, sticking

to the shadows. The Germans had forbidden all Poles to be out of doors after curfew hours which might be as early as six p.m. and never later than nine. He didn't say so, but he sighed gratefully that they had made the hazardous trip through the city safely. It was almost like a good omen.

Jan, still carrying Pawel, pushed the back door open with his shoulder. He explained, "There's no use locking it. The Gestapo only gets suspicious of locked doors if they come poking around."

Wanda followed him, holding her breath. Somehow, though strange and terrible things had happened to her during the two years since the Germans invaded Poland, she could never get quite used to the unnatural way she was living. Stealing across a sad, ruined city at night, hiding in alleyways and ruins when the night patrol tramped by, afraid to breathe, walking into a ghostly house that no longer belonged to anyone; it was still just as frightening as it had been during the first horrible days of war. She was homesick for safety.

Jan, ahead, suddenly whistled the opening bars of the "Polonaise":

Immediately, the last three notes echoed back.

"Jan?"

"It's me," Jan called softly. "Turn on the chandeliers. We have visitors."

"We're fresh out of matches," a cheerful voice said, "but wait."

There was a sound of a stove lid being lifted, and a warm red glow of coals gleamed into the room.

"A fire! You have a real fire!"

"*We* have a fire. It's yours too, and welcome. You're Wanda Denin, aren't you?" Stas had an irrepressible chuckle. "I always thought you were the prettiest girl in school."

"And this is Pawel." Jan carefully put Pawel down near a basket by the stove. He crawled into it happily.

Stas fastened a blanket over the window and lighted a candle from the coals. Wanda warmed her hands above the stove. Jan told the story of how they had met.

"You were perfectly right to bring them here," Stas said warmly.

Stas was a sturdy boy, shorter than Jan, with thick yellow hair that flopped around his ears and was a little too long at the neck. But despite the lack of a haircut he looked clean, and his gray eyes were direct and kind. His mouth looked ready to smile at any time. Wanda remembered that if you wanted anything practical done you'd ask him rather than Jan, who would immediately try to do it but wouldn't be half as good at it.

"And tomorrow we'll try to trace Pawel's family," Jan said.

The boys exchanged a worried look. There were hundreds of children left orphaned daily in Warsaw. The Nazi terror hadn't stopped with the occupation. Each day, more and more people were rounded up and sent to concentration camps, or shot in large groups and buried in a common grave they had had to dig themselves. The Germans seemed to have forgotten the Poles were humans. There was only a million-in-one chance of finding Pawel's family, particularly if they had been Jewish.

Wanda was saying softly, "It's wicked, I know, but I almost wish I didn't have to give him up. He's someone belonging to me because he needs me."

"I think there's still some soup left," Stas said. "I'm glad you are here, Wanda, because I'm the worst cook I ever knew."

Wanda slept long in the unaccustomed warmth by the stove.

When she woke up, a bit of the blanket by the window had been pulled back and greenish light came through the bushes outside the broken panes. On the kitchen table was a note.

Dear Guests, don't worry, we've only gone to look for Pawel's parents and get us a feast, we hope. Don't go out, Wanda. We'll be back soon. Stas and Jan.

P.S. There's some slightly moldy bread in the cupboard and a pail of water just outside the door. Don't bother trying the taps. They don't work. And don't eat Jan's delicious-looking glue. It makes him angry. He needs it in his secret service work. Stas.

Wanda laughed for the first time in a long time. Stas couldn't be downhearted whatever happened.

She found a kettle and heated some water. In the cupboard, she found almost half a loaf of bread. The boys were obviously better at scrounging food than she was. She cut two slices, a big one for Pawel and a little one for herself. She mashed Pawel's up in the warm water.

As she fed him, she could have cried at the thought of the milk he ought to be drinking, the fruit and porridge that would be so good for him. He was too little to remember the days of normal breakfasts, but she remembered.

"Good," said Pawel, smacking his lips. "Sunny shine too." He ran to the window. He thought this place was a great improvement on their recent dark cellar home. He wanted to go out.

But Stas and Jan had told them to wait inside. To keep Pawel occupied, Wanda decided to explore the house.

It must have been a pretty place before it was bombed, perhaps a riverside villa of someone who lived and worked in central Warsaw. The windows were long and well spaced, and had been patchily boarded up with old slabs of wood. Ragged curtains still hung from several of them. If she had needle and thread, Wanda thought, she could make a coat for Pawel from the better bits. But everything else that could be carried away had been stolen. Off the wide hall, at the back of the house was a room with faded yellow walls and an ornate rococo mantle. In a corner, on the floor, were two blanket rolls. Wanda felt guilty for having slept in the warm kitchen when she realized the boys must have camped here last night.

Beyond the salon, the house had caved in, and daylight streaked through the cracks in the wrecked stone and rubble.

The Germans hadn't requisitioned the house, Jan had explained, because it was such a complete mess. After they'd put their placard,

INSPECTED. DESERTED HOUSE.

on the door, the boys had moved in and scrounged bits and pieces from other ruins, for the kitchen.

Now there was a shout from the garden, "Wanda! Pawel!"

Stas came running to find them coming back from their exploration of the house.

"Riches!" he called. On the kitchen table, he was piling up eight potatoes, four turnips, two smoked herring, and a piece of bread. "And for Pawel," he said triumphantly, "sugar!"

"Not sugar! Where did you get it!"

16

"I liberated it from the Nazis!" said Stas gleefully. "I remembered my mother saying sugar was necessary for little kids. So it's for Pawel!"

"If I put a little bit of everything together and cook it slowly, it'll taste better and last longer," Wanda suggested. She'd learned a lot in the last lean two years. She wasn't even going to tell Stas not to take risks.

"And I'll go and find you some greens from the riverbank," Stas said.

They'd fed Pawel and he'd climbed back into his basket for an afternoon nap before Jan came back. They could tell nothing from his face.

"This does smell like a feast," he said.

"Please, Jan," Wanda said. "I can't eat anything until you tell us. What did you find out?"

Jan frowned. Then he said, keeping his voice matter-of-fact, "The day you found Pawel, his mother and father were taken by the Gestapo. His mother tried to run back to him. They shot her."

"How did you . . ." Stas began to ask.

Jan shook his head warningly. "*Stryj* Franek," he said briefly.

Whose uncle, Wanda wondered, whose uncle Franek?

Jan went over to Pawel's basket and stood looking down at the little boy. "They were very brave people," he said. "They had been working in the underground. They were Polish patriots. Pawel can be proud."

Perhaps the mention of his name reached

Pawel through sleep. He began to cry softly.

Jan knelt down and clumsily stroked the little boy's hair. "What is it?"

"My mummy's pwayer," Pawel sobbed. "Always at sleep time and I can't wemember it."

"Listen, Pawel," Jan said slowly, "I'll try to make you a new prayer. This can be Pawel's own prayer. You say it after me."

Pawel got up onto his knees.

Jan began, "I beg Thee, O Lord, to make me brave, and to help Poland win back her own dear land. Please, O Lord, take care of all who love Poland."

"And look after us all," Pawel added.

"Amen," they said.

3

The boy was in the middle of the kitchen before they'd even heard him enter. He was a small, thin boy with a dirty face that looked grim despite the turned-up nose and the freckles. His hair was cut so short he looked bald.

Wanda jumped up. "Who are you?"

The strange boy backed to the door.

Wanda spoke more softly, "Are they after you?"

The boy glanced over his shoulder. His voice was gruff. "I think I gave them the slip."

He looked like a street urchin from the slums. He was belligerent and dirty. There was always the river to wash in, Wanda thought to herself. But his angry manners might be because he was hungry. She remembered how it felt to be hungry. He was probably ten or eleven, and he was afraid. He was the sort of a boy she might never have met in the days of peace. But now *she* thought of only one thing. He was hungry.

She said, "Will you have some stew?"

Small Pawel had climbed out of his basket. "It's good stew," he said. "Potatoes."

"Does she mean it? I can have something to eat?" The boy turned to Jan.

"Yes, of course," Jan said. "What's your name?"

"Kazio."

Wanda had put a plateful on the table. The small boy began to wolf it, as though he thought someone would take it away from him. When he was nearly finished, he burped and began to talk.

"They were taking down the statue of Kilinski. One of them said they'd smash it to pieces. My father went out to try to stop them. We had homemade grenades. I was carrying some for him. He threw one and it didn't go off. They shot him. I threw mine and both went off. I saw two Germans go down. I ran. I didn't look back. I ran."

He slumped down at the table and buried his head into his arms.

"Is Kilinski a nice man?" Pawel had only understood the name.

Jan picked the child up and held him on his

lap. His voice was quiet. Somehow, in these tragic years, he'd learned to use a very matter-of-fact voice. "Jan Kilinski was a great patriot. He loved Poland. But above all, he loved the city of Warsaw. He was a shoemaker, and he lived a hundred and fifty years ago in the Old Town. In his time, too, an enemy held Warsaw. Kilinski led the people in a fight to free the city, and they won, and made him a statue. Throughout the years the citizens of Warsaw have revered and remembered him. That's the statue this boy says the Germans are demolishing."

Jan had talked slowly to give the boy time to pull himself together. Finally he lifted his head, and though his eyes were red, his voice was almost steady.

"My father is—was—a shoemaker too," he said. "My name is Kazio Kilinski. My father always said we might quite easily be related to the great Kilinski because we are in the same trade, and my grandfather before us, and others before him. *I'm going to get that statue!*"

"Sit down, Kazio," Jan said sternly. "Eat your soup. We can't take down and hide a big heavy statue. That's silly. But I'll go and find out if there is something we can do." He picked up his cap and went out.

"You can stay here tonight, Kazio," Stas said.

"Where has Jan gone?" Wanda asked.

"I can't tell you."

"Is it where you went last night?"

21

"How do you know we went out last night?"

"I heard you. Pawel was restless, and I was awake."

"We aren't supposed to talk about it," Stas said reluctantly. He didn't like keeping secrets from his friends. "But it has to do with work for Poland."

"Could I do it too?" Wanda cried.

"Can I help?" Kazio jumped up.

"I don't see why not," Stas said seriously. "But we'll have to ask first. What can you do, Kazio?"

"I can make shoes by hand just like my father and the great Kilinski," Kazio said. "I'll sneak back to our shop. I'll get my tools. Then I'll fix all your shoes."

"Me too?" Pawel asked.

"I'll make new ones for you," Kazio said. "I'll steal the leather somewhere."

He told them a lot of things about himself while they waited for Jan. It was dark before he returned. He slumped tiredly onto a chair.

"Nothing doing," he said. "The streets are full of the Gestapo."

"I'm doing something *tonight!*" Kazio shouted. "I'm a Kilinski too!"

Stas grabbed him as he flung open the door.

"My father," Kazio sobbed, "my father would have . . ."

The other three looked at one another. Of course, it was only today that Kazio had seen his own father killed. They didn't have to imagine how he felt. They remembered.

Jan carried sleepy Pawel into his basket. *Stryj* Franek hadn't exactly *forbidden* them to go out, he thought. He'd just said it was dangerous and unwise. Kazio was bound to do something silly tonight if they let him go alone.

"Listen, Kazio," he said. "We'll trust you. You can help us make the signs. Come on."

He lifted up a trap door under an old sacking in the corner of the kitchen.

Wanda stared, surprised. In her home there was her mother's maid and her father's valet and a governess and a maid for her. She had hardly ever seen the kitchen for it too was full of servants. But she did remember that the cold storage for vegetables, fruit, salted meat and fish was in the cellar. So this must be the same sort of a cellar.

Jan hauled on a rope and pulled up a ladder. Stas knelt down to help him.

"Wanda," Jan said, "please check that the curtains are drawn. Do not fasten the door. Should anyone come they would be suspicious about bolted doors. If they come we'll just be quiet. Stas, bring the candles, please. Now, come. Everyone."

Wanda looked back and saw that Pawel was fast asleep by the stove.

She followed the boys down the ladder into the cellar.

There was a table made of two long boards set on brick legs. The boys had scavenged what they needed from bombed houses. They'd made a couple of shelves along the wall—loaded with paint tins—and neatly stacked piles of paper and cardboard.

"We found the paint in a deserted shop," Jan explained. "Next to Stas's old home there used to be a stationery shop. When the Gestapo arrested the owner, they just threw everything around. He'd been our friend and given us paper and books before, so we knew he wouldn't mind if we saved what we could."

"That's why we're so well supplied," Stas added cheerfully. "We spent nights carting the stuff here."

"We'll make two signs," Jan said.

"THE PEOPLE OF WARSAW
WILL NOT FORGET JAN KILINSKI,
and
POLAND LIVES."

Kazio stood sullenly. "That's not enough." He swallowed a sob.

Wanda took his grubby hand. "Look, Kazio. It might not be much, but it'll annoy the Nazis terribly. And it'll cheer up the people of Warsaw."

Kazio stared at his feet. "I can't write," he mumbled.

"I'll block out the letters," Jan said. "You can start painting them."

"Anyone who can sew shoes, can paint," Stas said. "Get to work."

While they cut the cardboard for the signs, printed and painted, Jan told them he'd found out the Germans had removed the statue to the courtyard of the National Museum. The next day, it was to be "executed" as an example of what would happen to the Polish spirit of resistance, just as the statue of Chopin had been destroyed. It was the sort of horrifying, senseless gesture Germans liked. Like burning books that weren't pro-Nazi. They thought that to burn the book was to burn the idea in it.

It was nearly midnight, long past curfew time, when they finished.

"I'm taking them to Kilinski *now*," Kazio said.

Jan stared at him a long moment. "Well. I guess I'll have to come with you. But I tell you it's a stupid thing to do."

"Pawel's sound asleep," Wanda said. "I'm coming too."

It was a long way from their suburb to the National Museum. They hurried down the rubble-filled streets from shadow to shadow. They hid in the ruins when the night patrols tramped by. They were nearly there when Wanda slipped.

Jan and Stas, scouting ahead, didn't hear her gasp, but Kazio ran back to help. As he called to them in a loud whisper, they heard the menacing tramp again. The boys were already on their way

25

back. Ahead, the patrol was turning into the street.

There was nowhere to hide. The houses here were heaps of rubble and brick; the district was unfamiliar to them.

As the electric torches of the patrol flashed at them, a dark shadow moved between them and the light. Strong arms swept up Wanda. A low, deep voice ordered, "Here, boys," and pushed them through a dark broken doorway they hadn't seen in their panic.

The stranger led the way swiftly and quietly. They seemed to be passing through an archway, several houses, pitch-black passages. When they emerged into the moonlight again none of them knew where they were.

"Can you walk?" The stranger put Wanda down. "I know every beloved inch of Warsaw. Follow me."

They had no breath to ask where they were going. Yet, sooner than they could believe they found themselves climbing over the back wall of their own small garden. In the moonlight, under the bare trees, they saw the stranger quite plainly now.

He wore a long, cloaklike coat, fastened with a broad belt at the waist. His hat was like an end of a stocking, pulled down to his ears, and his hair hung down to his shoulders.

"Your intentions were good, my children," he said in a deep voice, "but you must take more care. Poland needs you alive."

26

Jan said, "Thank you, sir. We would have been caught but for you."

"Where ever did you come from, sir?" Stas sounded puzzled.

Kazio was trying to hold back his sobs. "We lost the signs, we lost our good signs."

"Never mind, Kazio Kilinski." The stranger rested a hand briefly on the small boy's shoulder. "They are not lost."

Lightly, he leaped over the stone wall, and they couldn't see him any more. They trailed into the house slowly, too tired even to talk. All of them were puzzled, except for Kazio who was sure he knew a wonderful secret.

Stas was gone when they woke up late the next morning. Wanda had fed Pawel and set out bread and cabbage soup for their breakfast when he returned.

"Look, I stole a whole large slab of salted ham. That cook in the Gestapo mess is half asleep in the mornings." He hauled the treasure from under his ragged jacket and slammed it on the table.

"Where have you been?" Jan said sternly.

"Just around." Stas reached for his bowl of watery soup. "I wanted to see where that doorway we went through last night was, for the next emergency. I couldn't find it. But," he grinned at them, "guess what?"

"Guess what, *what?*" they shouted at him.

"Guess what the Nazis are up to this morning?" He couldn't stop grinning. "Busy trying to scrub down a big sign. Painted right across the front of the National Museum two stories high. It must be awfully good paint because they can't get it off. And the letters are those archaic kind."

He stuffed his mouth with bread. His eyes sparkled.

"Stas! Stop teasing! What does it say?"

Stas jumped up and saluted them.

"In *big* letters it says:

I AM HERE, PEOPLE OF WARSAW.

"And right underneath:

JAN KILINSKI."

4

"We'll have to get organized," Jan said later that morning. "There are five of us now."

Kazio picked up his peaked cap and headed for the door.

"Where do you think you're going?"

"Five's too many." The boy turned his head away from them.

"Don't act silly. Where could you go?" Jan said. "Anyhow, I promised to teach you to write. How old are you?"

"I must be nearly eleven," Kazio said. "I remember my mama made me my eighth birthday cake. Before the bombings."

"And no school since the Germans came," Wanda said understandingly.

"We'll stick together," Jan said. "But let's not collect any more people. It isn't safe. And we must consult my uncle."

"*Stryj* Franek!" Wanda had heard the boys mention the name.

"That's right. He's pretty important. We can't see him often because it could be dangerous, but he'll advise us about Pawel and school and things like that."

"It was easier for you when it was only you and Stas."

Jan ignored such an obvious fact. "We'll have to scrounge for some blankets for Kazio."

"Could we go to my father's shop? They might not have taken everything. Like my tools." Kazio's lip trembled.

"We're with you," Stas said quickly.

"*Stryj* Franek will want to see you before I can tell you anything more." Jan picked up Pawel. "Let's go now."

"In the daytime?" Wanda was surprised. But Jan was already outside with Pawel perched on his shoulders.

As they followed him, Stas said, "Do you know what Jan's uncle did before the war?" He began to laugh. "He was a professor of philosophy at the University."

"What's so funny about that?" Wanda demanded. But Stas only kept laughing.

She was even more puzzled when they headed for the Saxon Park, once the playground for Warsavians. But now German headquarters flanked the gardens. Why was Jan heading there— Jan, who was always preaching about not taking risks.

It was warm for early April and Pawel kept up a little song about how hot his coat was. Wanda let her patched, too-small overcoat hang open. The boys debated where they could "find" some shirts to replace their worn-out sweaters.

In Saxon Park, the grass was already turning green though the trees were still bare. Stas had been clever to find edible river greens so early, Wanda thought; perhaps, soon there would be something else growing to replace the winter-frosted potatoes and moldy cabbage. Although, she added quickly in her mind, they'd been lucky to have had those.

Unexpectedly, Jan stopped beside a tall, lean man who was industriously sweeping the walks.

"This is Wanda, *Stryj* Franek," he said in a low voice, "and Pawel, and Kazio."

A professor of philosophy who worked as a street cleaner, Wanda stared at him open-mouthed. Stas was bent double with laughter. The tall man smiled, and Pawel immediately went to him and reached for his hand.

"This is an excellent way for me to get fresh air and exercise, child, and do the work I must do now," he said in a low voice, "until we all go back to our own proper jobs again."

He didn't have to say more. They knew that the Germans had closed all Polish schools, and either shot or sent to concentration camps all the teachers and intellectuals they had been able to track down. The only ones who had escaped were those who had had time to take on other identities —pretend to be someone else but themselves.

Jan's uncle had given her a long, intent look. Now he turned and looked at Kazio just as carefully. Then he began to sweep the path again, moving away from them.

Wanda said anxiously, "I know Jan and Stas are working for Poland. I'd like to have a useful job too."

"There will be duties for you all," the tall man said very softly. "Go now."

"Come on, come on," Jan said anxiously. "Wanda. Kazio. Where's Pawel?"

The tall man was moving slowly down the path. The little boy was nowhere in sight. He'd vanished like quicksilver.

"There are Germans everywhere around here," Jan hissed. "Find him, quick. We're only safe if we are moving."

"Scatter," Stas said. "He can't have got far."

They hadn't taken many steps when they heard the song. The tune was Jan's beloved "Polonaise Militaire."

32

But the words were entirely unexpected.

"Day will come when we will wash with
  Soap again,"

a clear voice was singing behind a high clump of bushes. A piping chorus repeated the last bar:

"Soap again!"

The song went on:

"Day will come when we will have warm
  Baths again.
  Baths again."

There was Pawel's toneless little voice joining in.

"They must be crazy," Jan said stormily. "In this district!"

He pushed through the hedge. The others followed. There, by a tap where the gardeners fastened their hoses when there was water, was a thin girl with fair pigtails washing the very dirty hands of two identical little girls. Close to them, crouched down, was Pawel. He was trying to catch the trickle of water in his cupped palms.

"What do you mean putting words like that to Chopin's music," Jan stormed. "It's sacrilege!"

33

The song died in midair. The girl stared at him, wide-eyed. Then she laughed. "I know I'm no poet," she said.

"And you must be mad too," Jan continued, "singing Chopin where the Germans can hear you. They've forbidden it. If you don't care about yourself, think of them."

He gestured at the frightened-looking little girls.

"Have you ever tried washing tiny hands in freezing water with sand?" the girl snapped. Then she added, placatingly, "But you are right. I am sorry. Only we found this water and I just didn't think."

She picked up two ragged little coats and put them on the two small girls. They had short black hair, with bangs across their foreheads.

They looked so alike Wanda couldn't help asking, "They're twins, aren't they?"

"Yes. Jadwika and Ludwika," the girl said, "and I am Marja."

Wanda was about to introduce everyone when Jan picked up Pawel and said shortly, "We have to go now."

"Are you all one family?" the girl asked wistfully.

"No," Wanda said. "We just live together."

They hurried through the park. Marja and the twins followed.

Jan threw a dark look at them. He felt a little ridiculous about his outburst and he didn't like

34

feeling ridiculous. All the same, in his heart he was sure you shouldn't put Chopin's music to anything but the noblest of words.

They crossed the street. Still Marja and the twins followed them.

From his perch on Jan's shoulders, Pawel kept waving a friendly hand at Jadwika and Ludwika. They waved back.

Jan's face got stormier and stormier as they turned down their own street and still the three trailed behind. Stas hid his smile. Wanda was longing to talk to the oddly self-contained girl, but that seemed disloyal to Jan.

As they turned in at the pillared half ruin that Wanda was already calling "home" in her own mind, the three remained behind on the street, holding hands, staring after them.

Stas started to light the fire in the kitchen. He looked over his shoulder at Jan. "What are you going to do about them?"

"Nothing. We have enough to cope with."

"The little girls looked cold and hungry," Wanda said. "We could put more potatoes in the soup, and a slice of Stas's ham. We've bread. And warm water for them to wash."

"And have them stay here forever?" Jan said. "No."

"That Marja looked thin as a herringbone," Stas said.

"Her shoes were all broken," Kazio said suddenly. "I could fix them."

"All right, all right," Jan shouted. "Invite all Warsaw!"

He threw open the kitchen door. Right behind it stood Marja and the twins. Their faces looked a little scared, a little hopeful.

Wanda went swiftly to them and pulled the little girls in. "I'm no good as a cook, Marja," she said. "Won't you come and help me with this stew."

"Potato soup." Marja sniffed happily. "Have you an onion because if not I've been saving this one for an occasion."

She pulled an onion out of her pocket and picked up a knife.

"Day will come when we can eat
Enough again . . ."

"Groan!" said Jan loudly. He threw open the trap door to the cellar. "Come on, Stas, we've work to do."

"What's the matter with him?" Cutting the onion, stirring the soup, Marja seemed quite sure of herself. As though she'd always lived with them, Wanda thought, wondering who she was and where she really lived.

"Jan loves Chopin's music," Wanda explained gently. "He used to be the top student at the Music Academy even though he wasn't the oldest, before . . ."

"I know. Before everything changed. All right, I'll try to remember, though I rather think

Chopin would be pleased to know his music cheers us up just as much as it makes us feel patriotic."

Jan's head suddenly disappeared below the trap door. The girls hadn't seen him, but he'd heard.

"Where are you living?" Wanda couldn't help her curiosity.

"Nowhere." Marja bent down to help the twins out of their coats. "Do you mind if we don't talk about it now."

She sounded stiff and old-fashioned, but Wanda nodded. There had been many times in the past two years she hadn't wanted to talk either.

The stew was nearly ready and smelling succulent when Jan and Stas climbed back into the kitchen and closed the trap door.

"Look, Pawel," Jan said. "An ABC Book for you and Kazio and the twins."

Then, very casually, he sang:

"Day will come when we will have real
  Books again.
  Books again."

5

At dusk, several days later, Jan's uncle came to see them.

He dropped onto a kitchen chair with a sigh. He looked thin and tired, but when he lifted his head and smiled, Pawel and the twins ran to lean against his knees.

"Here, little ones." He pulled a handful of dried apple slices from his pocket. From his other pocket, he produced a small paper bag of flour and two tins of powdered milk. "Now that your family includes so many babies we'll have to try to see if we can find something for them from time to time."

"That's wonderful." Wanda realized Jan must have been to see his uncle and told him about Marja and the twins. "I've really been worried. I do know the little ones ought to have more nourishing food."

"All the Polish babies lack the simplest necessities these days. All we can do is to pray and work for freedom and victory before it's too late for them."

Jan looked worriedly at his uncle. It was unheard of for *Stryj* Franek to sound discouraged.

"Is anything wrong?" he asked anxiously.

Stryj Franek straightened his shoulders. "There are so many things wrong in our dear Poland these days that we must tackle one task at a time. To have food to survive is, of course, important, but just as important is that you children grow up worthy of the Free Poland we will surely live to see. Jan, how much schooling have you had since the occupation?"

"You know well, my uncle," Jan stammered, "that my school was closed by the Nazis two months after they came. Then I had lessons whenever possible at Professor Zielinski's house until they sent him to the concentration camp. That's all. And music—I haven't played at all."

"Two and a half years with no schooling," Stryj Franek said gravely. "You do realize this is according to the German Plan. We have seen their secret orders: *'Polish children must grow up uneducated, only fit for slave labor.'* That was the reason they closed all our schools and universities. Then they took over, destroyed our theatres, museums, libraries, bookstores, and publishing houses. The ignorance they are trying to force on all our children and young people is what we must fight."

"We've tried!" Stas cried. "We snooped around our old schools trying to find books. We've gone through the ruins of the libraries. What they haven't stolen and carted away to Germany they've burned. The few books we found, we took."

"What were you going to study, Stas?"

"I wanted to be an engineer, like my father. I wanted to build bridges, and dams, and new cities such as Gdynia out of the marshes. I was going to go to University to learn how. My father and mother were both killed in the September twenty-fifth raid. I didn't go back to school. Jan found me and he's taught me some things, but he doesn't know about engineering."

"And you, little Kazio?"

"I didn't like school." The small boy looked sullen. "I used to stay away and help my father in our shop. I never had music lessons like Wanda, and Stas, and Jan. I thought kids like that were soft. They aren't. They're fine. But if it's going to make the Germans mad, I'll learn to read, and I'll learn everything else Jan'll teach me."

Stryj Franek put out his hand to Kazio. "That's fine, my son. We can defeat the Germans by learning more than we ever learned before. And all of us, every Pole, must take part in that campaign."

He couldn't tell the children that his deep sadness and anxiety that evening was due to the information the underground headquarters had just received. From all over Poland, the figures had been sent and tabulated and were now known to be authentic. Of course they had known that in the short September 1939 campaign over 800,000 Polish soldiers had died. But since then, the Germans occupying Poland had executed, murdered, killed in concentration camps, prisons, and gas chambers over four million civilian Poles. Before victory was won and peace came, more would die, perhaps these children among them. And yet the Western world found it impossible to believe the unbelievable atrocities of the Nazis. But one day, truth would prevail.

Meanwhile hope could only live in endeavor. *Stryj* Franek knew he must give the children faith in their task and in themselves.

"But what can we do!" Jan cried bitterly. "We haven't even anything to read. A little makeshift ABC we made for the little ones."

"There are still books hidden which I will get and lend to you," *Stryj* Franek said. "And you must share the knowledge with as many children as you can. The ABC was a splendid start."

"You mean *we'll* write something." Jan was staring at his uncle, his eyes brightening. "Why, we could write a newspaper! An underground paper for children, the way adults have their underground news sheets! Is that what you mean?"

The bigger children gathered close to the tall, thin man now. Their faces were eager, but he looked at them gravely. "You do know that if the Germans discover what you are doing, you'll be shot."

"We know," they said, but it was as though a freezing blast had blown through the kitchen.

"You still want to go on with it?"

"Yes," they said, one after another. "Yes, we do."

"Well then," *Stryj* Franek said briskly, "the underground will help you all we can. Have you any ideas yourselves?"

"We've got quite a lot of paper still," Stas said, "but we could do with a printing press."

Kazio stood up. He said shyly, "Next to my father's shop there used to be a small print shop. When I went to get my tools the other day, I looked in. It was wrecked, of course, but there was a small, old handpress in the cellar. It's rusty, but it could be fixed. In the Other Days, I used to help the Old Man set type."

"Would he let us have it?"

"He was a Jew," Kazio said. "They took him away."

"We'll bring it here to our workshop," Stas said.

"No. That would be unwise. You must not do anything in the place where you live. You must also remove the paper and paints you have here now, and find another place for your newspaper office. Should the Germans search here, the place must seem simply and innocently a shelter for children."

Stryj Franek got up and stretched himself wearily. He picked up his broom by the doorway and smiled. "Come, cheer up. *All together we cannot fail.*"

His smile embraced them all.

"Come to think of it," he added, "it would be safer if the girls and Pawel used the loft under the eaves, in the unbombed wing, now that warmer weather is coming. You could pull the ladder up after you and put it out again from the window to the garden. In the summer the lilac bushes will hide it. God keep you all."

"How did he know about the loft upstairs?" Wanda wondered. "He didn't ever go out of the kitchen."

"Didn't I tell you?" Jan smiled. "This is his house. That's why the Nazis blew it up. But they didn't do a very good job of it, thank goodness."

All the little household sang words to the "Polonaise Militaire" these brightening spring days. Wanda would hum it as she made Jadwika and Ludwika stick to their alphabet. Kazio, not wanting to "learn with babies," had made a tremendous effort to remember what he had once known and could already read, though slowly, the few children's books Jan had brought from *Stryj* Franek.

And when he was patching the broken soles, and fixing the heels of everybody's ragged shoes, he would sing:

> "Day will come when all will buy new
> Shoes again . . ."

And Stas, printing extra pages for the primer, would sing:

"Day will come when I can get some
Ink again . . ."

Most of the days, however, the boys were out searching for a safe "office." It was on the day they found it that the "Polonaise" gained added meaning to them.

They had been burrowing like moles through the ruins of the Old Town. This day they had explored the bombed shells and cellars of the once charming neoclassic buildings that had lined the market square. There were enough tunnels and passages, underground halls and cellars, to have hidden an army; though, perhaps safe from the Germans, they had been so badly bombed they were unsafe for occupation. The Old Town walls bordered the square and it was under its sturdy strength that they found a room that seemed perfect for their office.

Above it was a wilderness of buttresses, archways, and rubble-heaped passages, but they figured they could clear a secret entrance to the still sturdy, stone-roofed room. Better yet, they could make an emergency exit through the deserted ruin on the other side.

They would need shovels and brooms from home to start the cleaning up, but on the way, they decided to have a look at the hand press.

It was not safe for the boys to walk together. The Germans were suspicious of "gangs." So Kazio was ahead, showing the way.

He looked back as he turned into a lane.

A second later a sharp urgent whistle rang out. The "Polonaise."

Immediately, Jan turned back. Stas had stopped by a buttress that arched the street. They didn't need words. They scrambled up the broken bricks. There was no time to go further. They threw themselves down on the flat top. Not a moment too soon.

The cobblestoned street below them thundered with heavily booted feet. Bullets smacked at the walls. The German shouts echoed from the stones. And then there was a high dreadful scream.

"Not us," Jan whispered, white-faced. "A hunt."

There was no need to say anything more. The frequent Nazi "hunts" were a punishment for some specially daring act of sabotage, or, often, just to remind the people of Warsaw who was the boss now. Without warning truckloads of soldiers would pour into any section of the city and round up everyone they caught on the streets. It didn't matter to the Germans whom they shot, innocent or guilty, even women and children. The Poles had learned to recognize the sounds of a hunt, and hide.

In a few minutes the chase, the shouting, and shooting had passed on. But Jan and Stas

46

waited before they peered down from the roof. There was no one in sight. The old walls of Warsaw had sheltered at least some of their own, again.

"Where's Kazio?" Jan whispered. "If he hadn't warned us . . ."

"Not such a little boy," Stas said despairingly. "Surely they wouldn't . . ."

"You know they would. But I am going to find him—dead or alive."

Dusty and scratched, angry, they dropped to the street below. As they picked themselves up, a slight figure flashed around the corner and was at them like a happy terrier.

"Kazio!" They hugged one another in their burst of relief.

"What happened?"

"They were piling out of their trucks at the end of the lane when I came around the corner. There was no time to go back. So I whistled, jumped into the first doorway, and hid inside a heap of rubbish."

"What made you think of the 'Polonaise'?"

"What 'Polonaise'? I whistled the tune we sing at home. I knew you'd get it."

"Oh, Kazio, you little moron," Jan said. "Let's go home and tell everyone how really smart you are."

Everyone made much of Kazio that evening. He wouldn't take an extra helping of food, but he was awfully pleased with himself, particularly when Jan told him that the "Polonaise" was as much a part of the brave spirit of Poland as the great Kilin-ski himself.

"It's practically the song of Poland," Jan told him. "Why, the Radio Warsaw played it again and again when the city was under bombardment, just these first bars. I don't know who ordered it to be played, or who played it, but it certainly put heart into all who heard it."

"One day you will play the whole thing to us, Jan?" Kazio asked.

"One day," Jan said.

The frightening incident didn't stop them from going back to the Old Town. Every night for a week the boys carried parts of the press, the type, printing ink, paper, and other supplies to the secret room in the walls which they now importantly called "The Office." They swept and cleaned and secured their entrance and exit. They made tables and chairs from packing cases and old barrels they scrounged from the ruins. *Stryj* Franek sent a man to help them put the press together and show them how it worked.

Wanda and Marja felt quite out of it. Surely they could do more than just look after the little ones, try to patch up everybody's clothes, and cook.

"Let's go on strike if they don't let us help," Marja said.

"Let's wait just a few days more," said Wanda, who knew Jan better.

48

And sure enough, one evening Jan said, "We will now hold an editorial conference."

Pawel and the twins were already in bed, so the Big Five, who had come together so strangely, gathered around the kitchen table.

"The first thing on the agenda," Jan said, "is, what will we call our newspaper?"

"How about 'Liberty,' or 'Freedom'?" Wanda asked.

For half an hour they argued back and forth (Kazio's contribution was "Kilinski"), but nothing seemed just right.

"Maybe this is silly," Marja said at last, "but I think it shouldn't have a name at all, but a *meaning*."

"Go on. What do you mean?"

"Well . . ." she reached for a piece of paper. "I'd just like to have the first notes of the 'Polonaise,' right across the top of the first page, like this":

They watched as she quickly wrote down the first bars of the tune they now considered their very own, and Wanda found herself thinking that they knew nothing at all about Marja. They didn't know where she came from, or her last name. They hadn't known she could play, much less write, music. She'd just never volunteered to talk about herself.

Jan was staring thoughtfully at the line of music. Kazio's eyes were popping with surprise. He'd never seen music written before.

"If that's our song," he said, his urchin face flushed with excitement, "I like it fine. Lots of kids like me who'll be too scared to *shout* a warning will learn to *whistle* a warning. My daddy told me that in the ancient days the people of Warsaw shouted the name of Kilinski when they fought for freedom. This would be sort of the same thing, wouldn't it?"

"But what will we *call* it," Jan worried.

Wanda sang out suddenly:

"Time will come when Poland will be
   Free again!"

"Free again!"

the rest sang out.

"The motion is unanimously carried," Jan said. "Now, the next thing is, we won't be able to do it all by ourselves."

"But we don't want to endanger others," Wanda said.

"We'll have to whether we like it or not," Jan said. "We'll need help in distributing it. There's no point in printing a paper and not getting it to people to read. Stas and I used to take the 'Freedom News' around for the underground until just a short time ago when *Stryj* Franek said we were getting too well known on the streets."

"I can do it," Kazio said.

"We can all do it," Stas said, "but we won't be enough."

Kazio said, "I know a lot of boys. They used to live on my street. I see some of them in the market square, and around, still. In the Other Days, we used to have two gangs and play Indian wars on the river flats. I could get them to deliver the paper."

"Splendid," Jan said. Small boys like Kazio were like flies, everybody was so used to them they'd be practically invisible.

He didn't really like to give the younger boys such a dangerous assignment, but he knew, and *Stryj* Franek had repeatedly warned them, that they, at fourteen and fifteen years of age, were too big to be seen on the streets too often. Most of Stas's and his friends had already been picked up and sent to work camps, unless their parents had been able to spirit them away somewhere to relatives or friends in the country.

So Jan sighed, clapped Kazio on the shoulder and said, "You'll be the boss. Pick out the best of your gang, Kazio. Quick-witted, fast, dependable. Tell them it's dangerous before you tell them anything else."

"Will their mothers let them do it?" Wanda said softly. What would her own gentle mother have thought of all this! She knew. She added, "They will. Because it'll be for Poland."

51

"Now all we have to do is to write the paper." Stas grinned. "That's all."

"I've written the editorial for the first number." Jan flushed. He wasn't as sure of himself as he liked to pretend. "To explain why there is going to be a children's underground paper."

"Read it to us."

Jan shuffled his papers. He cleared his throat. Then he read:

> "The Germans want us to forget about the glory of Poland. They want us to think as slaves, to grow up to be their slaves. Never forget, children of Poland, you have a right to be proud of your land, proud of her long and valiant history."

"Hey, wait a minute," Stas said. "I've an idea. Why don't we help everybody to remember Poland's history."

"How do you mean?"

"Remember the way children's magazines used to have competitions before the occupation, when we had magazines? Well, why don't we have a historical quiz. All about Duke Henry who defeated the Tartars and saved all Europe. And Copernicus whom all the world reveres: why? And King Jan Sobieski who saved Vienna: how and when? And the Third of May Constitution and everything."

"How would we get their answers?" Wanda asked practically.

"They'll give it to the kids who'll deliver the

papers. The readers will be bound to get to know them in time. It'll be a risk, but it'll be worth it. To prove it can be done right under the Germans' noses."

"We could give a prize of something to eat to the winner," Marja sighed, "saved from our own food."

"No," Jan said. "A contest would be too dangerous. An unnecessary risk. I think it's a good idea to have a story or two in every issue about brave Poles from our history. Then we can also write down the rules the adult underground uses. You know—don't look at Germans, ignore them. If they ask you for directions, say you don't know, or give wrong ones. If they send you on a message, pretend you are stupid and deliver it to a wrong place, or don't deliver it at all. If you understand German, pretend you don't. Things like that."

"I can think of a lot more," Marja said, and began to scribble on a piece of paper.

"Then I think we should write stories about the Poles fighting outside Poland with the Allied Forces, to encourage the Poles here at home. *Stryj* Franek's told me a couple of good ones about boys just sixteen and seventeen," Jan said.

"I think we should use that prayer you made up for Pawel," Wanda said. "There are thousands of orphan children in Warsaw alone. They'd be glad to have a prayer too if they've forgotten their old ones."

Several hours later, tired but still enthusiastic, they realized they'd thought up enough material for not only one, but quite a few newspapers.

"And at the very end," Marja said, as they got up to go to bed, "couldn't we put the words of the Polish National Anthem:

> Poland is not yet lost
> While still we live . . ."

"Yes," Jan said. "We'll use that."

7

Jan had corrected the first proofs of the first issue. Now the little handpress was rolling, Marja feeding paper into it, Kazio turning the crank, Wanda taking up the sheets and folding them. Stas was making bundles.

"Make them small enough to slip inside a shirt or coat." Jan went to help him.

A candle fluttered on the plank between two barrels that Jan used as a table. Curled up in a barrel chair Pawel was sound alseep, but Ludwika and Jadwika were still lisping over their alphabet books. The older children had come to the office early, and had been working all day, so the little ones had had to come too.

Kazio gave a final flip to the handle.

It was then the lame boy arrived, like a ghost from the shadows.

He was a thin, gangly boy, his curling hair long, his gray eyes deep set, his thin hands tight about his crutches.

"So there really is an underground paper," he said.

"How did you get here?" Jan stepped forward threateningly. Stas and Kazio moved up behind him.

Their secret place had been discovered. All was lost even before they had got started.

"Stop worrying," the lame boy said. "I wasn't followed. Nobody notices me. But I see everything because I watch."

"What do you want?"

"I heard about the paper," the boy said. "I just wanted to make sure it wasn't a German trap. I am Stefan." He looked at them steadily. "OK. I see it's for real," he said finally. "I'll tell the others. And I'll help you."

"What do you mean, you'll tell the others?" Jan demanded. "What others?"

"*My* chums," lame Stefan said. "We know that you and your friends went to the good schools and took music and painting, and got prizes. You're safe but Kazio is from the quarter of working people. How do we know we can trust him or

56

his friends. He might like the Russians, even if he doesn't like the Nazis. Me and my friends, we are just ordinary, but we are Poles, and if we want to help you you can't stop us. But we want to be sure about Kazio."

"Why, you, you!!" Kazio leaped at the lame boy. "I am a Kilinski!"

Stas caught him and held him back.

"Kazio is our friend," Jan said stiffly. "I want to know more about *you*."

"The kids trust me. Probably because of these." He tapped his crutches. "They consult me. A lot of them have come to me about this distribution business. That's why I'm checking."

"You thought this might be a German trap," Jan said slowly. "Yet you came here?"

"Sure. What have I to lose? And believe me, nobody else knows of this place. It took even me quite a time to nose it out."

"How did you think you could help?"

"I thought I'd manage the depot, the spot where the kids will collect the papers. Most of them know me anyhow, and it's safer if they don't meet you. Safer for the paper. I don't care about you." He looked at Kazio. "You. I hear you're using your father's old shop as the depot. Well, start carrying the papers there. I'll deal with it from that point on."

"Wait," Jan said. "You seem to have already messed up *our* plans. How are *you* going to set up the distribution now?"

"The kids are around, hiding. I'll whistle them up. Get cracking, Kazio. Or I'll be there before you."

He gave them a sudden extraordinarily sweet smile and his voice was completely different. "I'll be back to report on progress, Chief."

"I suppose we'll have to trust him," Jan said uneasily.

"He is putting on the tough-guy act," Marja said.

"I think I've heard about him," Kazio said slowly. "Stefan the lame boy. He is sort of a leader, I should have remembered about him. He's suspicious of everyone. That's probably why he was so hard on me. I am going to take the papers to my father's shop, just as we planned."

"I'm going to bring a couple of loads too," Stas said. "I'll check on him."

They stuffed small bundles of the paper inside their shirts and picked up the ragged potato sacks they had filled.

"Good luck," Jan said, tight-lipped.

Wanda glanced at him. She knew he was longing to take his chances with them, but they had decided against it. His main task was to edit the paper.

Kazio skirted a maze of passages and backyards. He had planned their route so carefully there was only one big street to cross. Stefan was already waiting for them. Stas and Kazio went back for another load of papers, and he took over.

His shrill whistle brought in eager workers, children of all sizes, ragged and thin.

"Helena, Wladyslas, Witold, Bronislaw, Irena," Stefan said, "each of you take two bundles. You know your routes. Be careful. Be quick."

Death was in every issue of the simple little paper. All the children knew that. But they snatched up the bundles and were on their way. When Kazio and Stas came up with the next load, Stefan had another gang ready.

Down the streets of Warsaw ran the ragged children. There were grins on their faces and comradeship in the hurried glances they exchanged as they passed one another.

Helena, her black hair swinging, skipped down the street. She didn't stop skipping when a Storm Troop patrol marched by. She didn't stop skipping when she passed the guards by the German Officers Club. She skipped all the way to the street Stefan had told her was her responsibility. It was close to her own school and she remembered that in the corner house there had lived a family with many children. She had used to stop to play with the babies in the Other Days.

Now she ran up the steps, slipped a paper through the letter slot and skipped away again. She did not know that the babies had died from lack of food, the father was fighting with the Polish forces in Africa, and the mother was sick with despair. Now the woman who had meant to die was staring at the bar of "Polonaise," reading Jan's brave words, and thinking, with a tug of hope in her heart, "All is not lost, after all. Our children haven't given up."

Wladyslas met his first customer on the street. He was small but pugnacious, so he didn't back up when the big, sullen boy blocked his way. He fished a copy of the paper from inside his jacket and said, "Read that. If you want to help, be here tomorrow."

And the sullen, lonely boy sat down on the curb and began to read, and thought to himself, "Why, there *is* something I can do after all."

Witold was fourteen. If he'd been in America, he'd have been a quiz kid. He was full of information about everything.

He had been given a difficult assignment. It was a street of apartment houses. If you happened to hand the paper to a wrong person, Stefan had warned him, it wouldn't be easy to escape. He decided to leave a paper at every second flat. If there happened to be only adults there, surely they'd pass it on to children. He ran quickly up and down the staircases and down the halls, sticking the little paper through the cracks between the floor and the door.

Behind one of those doors a man was hiding. He had escaped from a Nazi prison train on way from one concentration camp to another. His nerve was broken and he had decided to give himself up, stop running, tell all he knew. Even Wi-

60

told's light footsteps in the corridor made him jump.

He read every word of the paper, and then he read it again. "The *children* haven't given up," he thought. "We cannot fail them. Of course I must keep on fighting."

Bronislaw's beat was on a street that was full of children. He ran down it like the Pied Piper of Hamelin, handing out the paper, answering questions, swaggering a little because he felt happy and important. He forgot to hide his bundle of papers.

He ran right into a Gestapo patrol that marched out of a side street. One of the soldiers got hold of his shoulder.

"Scram," he shouted, but already the other children had scattered.

Bronislaw wriggled out of his jacket and ran. And then a shot rang out and he crumbled on the pavement. One of the Nazis kicked at him and saw he was dead. Another picked up the little paper.

"Underground publication," he snapped. "Bring the body. We'll search it."

They stepped on the papers that had fallen from Bronislaw's hands. They didn't bother to pick them up.

After they had gone, a girl sneaked out of a doorway. Fearfully, hastily, she collected the little papers, smoothed them against her knee. She picked up every one and ran off.

Irena was sent to the outskirts of Warsaw. Under tall pine trees were low wooden houses the

Nazis had thought too humble to occupy. She knew that some Polish nurses and nuns had organized an improvised hospital there for sick children. She knocked on the door.

A woman with a kind, tired face opened it. Irena curtsied.

"Sister," she said, "I'm delivering a children's underground paper. I was told to tell you that it would be dangerous to be found with a copy, but I thought perhaps the sick children . . ."

"Come in, child." The nurse put her arm around Irena's shoulder. "Your paper is welcome here. It is as important to be healed in mind as in body."

Meanwhile, in the cellar room under the old walls, Jan, Wanda, Marja and Stas were frowning in their effort to think up new ideas for the next issue of the paper, and Kazio ran back and forth bringing Lame Stefan's report of what was happening in the city. When they were ready to stop, Kazio came back once more to say that more copies were needed. So they started printing, and folding and tying up the bundles again.

They were still slow and clumsy. Even their bones ached with tiredness by the time Jan finally called a halt.

"We'll go home now," he said wearily, rubbing his eyes with a hand that smeared printer's ink all over his face.

The stars were fading and there was a faint stripe of dawn in the eastern sky. Jan, carrying

Pawel, led the way through the shadows.

Wanda, bringing up the rear, had a sudden strange vision. She seemed to see the curving, cobbled streets, the old squares, and the wide parks alive with children. Children like herself, and Jan and Marja, and Stas, and Kazio slipping from shadow to shadow, hiding from the cruel, incomprehensible enemy, delivering freedom papers, painting brave, loyal signs on the bombed walls, helping one another, singing.

That singing puzzled Wanda. She couldn't understand how they could sing the "Polonaise" and the National Anthem so loudly and not be caught. And then she realized it was only the humming in her ears, and the sound of the River Vistula flowing to the sea, and Stas, carrying one of the twins, whistling very quietly under his breath.

She was almost asleep as she stumbled on, helping Jadwika, to the ruined building that was home, now. The birds were beginning to awaken when they finally got to bed.

8

Though Bronislaw's death sobered the children, it did not stop the work on the paper. The second issue had come out two weeks after the first, the third a week later, and now they were turning out one issue punctually each week.

Every few days, Stefan reported that new children had contacted him, asking how they could help. The mothers and fathers sent messages too: "We will help you all we can," and, "Here's a small sum of money to help you carry on." They feared for their children, but they were ready to take risks to keep hope alive.

The paper was some sort of assurance that

young Poland would not grow up uneducated and stultified by Nazi propaganda. It gave the children a chance to participate in active resistance, stirred their imagination, and gave them incentive for more study. The parents were unanimous in their belief that whatever the risks, the effort was most worthwhile.

All the money that was sent to them Jan gave to *Stryj* Franek. The underground provided them with a supply of paper, printing ink, and other necessities as well as advice and stories from the world outside.

There were many things Jan could not write—nothing that could give any information to the Germans should the paper fall into their hands. But their way of delivering the paper was so well organized now that word-of-mouth messages, or warnings, could reach thousands of children during a day's distribution. One day, an exciting message came to *them*.

Jan, Marja and Stas were in the office under the walls that day. Wanda had taken Pawel and the twins to a welfare center where occasionally there was milk available for the very little children. Kazio brought the news. He'd run all the way.

"There's a boy," he gasped breathlessly. "He's blind. He wants to talk to you, Jan. He's got news."

"Where is he?"

"I left him at Stefan's. It's about a new German airfield, outside Warsaw, all camouflaged and everything."

"Fetch *Stryj* Franek, Stas," Jan said. "Kazio, you bring the boy here. This is something we can't handle alone. Be careful."

"I can't concentrate any more." Marja had been writing a story for small children, to be printed in the paper. "It *is* exciting, all the new things we are hearing about. Like the girl who told Stefan how she and her sister sneak down to the Vistula shore and untie the mooring ropes of German boats. And the girl from the village who sent in a story about how all the children on the farms turn signposts to point in wrong directions to mislead the Germans."

"Which reminds me," Jan said, "have you written up the latest score on punctured automobile and bicycle tires?"

"All right, I'll write it," Marja laughed. "How silly it sounded when Stas first thought of a Puncture-German-Tires-Brigade."

"But the results aren't silly," Jan said. "And there's nothing the Nazis can do about it. I think Kazio's squad is going to win the prize again."

There was a soft whistle at the secret entrance and Kazio led in a small, brown-haired boy. His eyes were wide open, but they didn't focus anywhere. Yet he walked very surely as though he trusted Kazio to lead him well.

"This is Michal," Kazio said.

"Let us tell Michal who we are," Marja said

quickly, and took his hand. "I am Marja. I have pigtails. Jan is tall and dark and he looks angry when he is serious, but he really isn't. Kazio has red hair and he is very clever at doing things."

Michal laughed with pleasure. "Thank you, Marja. Jan, this is what I know." He was serious now. "There are deep woods behind our farm. Though I've never been able to see, I've walked there all my life. There are many paths, and I can hear the wild animals hurrying about their business. I found, years ago, a meadow hidden in the forest. The day before yesterday I went there to look for spring greens. Usually, it is quiet in the woods, so quiet you can only hear the animals and even your own breathing. This time I kept hearing strange sounds. When I came to the edge of the clearing there were strong sounds of people shouting and of engines and whistles. I didn't go beyond the trees. I went home as fast as I could. My feet know the path well."

Michal took a long breath. "My father and two brothers fled with the army to Hungary. At home, there are only my grandfather and me. My mother was in Warsaw during the bombing and we never saw her again. I told Grandfather what I'd heard. His foot has been bad, but yesterday he took his stick and came with me. This is what we saw."

It didn't seem funny to the children that Michal should say "saw." His blindness was a handicap he'd conquered. Now he whirled about.

"Who's there?" he demanded.

The other children hadn't even heard *Stryj* Franek come in.

"I heard most of your story from the steps, Michal," he said. "Go on with it."

Michal stood very quietly for a long moment. Then he nodded to himself, as though satisfied, and took some stones and sticks from his pocket. "These help me to remember," he explained.

In separate heaps, he piled up larger stones, medium-sized ones, little ones, and the sticks.

"Grandfather counted four high-ranking officers." Michal pushed four large stones forward. "He says my meadow has been flattened and made into runways. These sticks are buildings. There are trees and branches on the roofs, so even if Allied planes flew over they could not see anything. Grandfather counted eleven large buildings—some looked like airplane hangars, some like barracks, and a couple were guarded. He counted forty airplanes, and there could have been more, inside, or in the air. These little stones are other officers he counted. He thinks this is probably the place from where German attacks on the Russian-held territories are launched. Some of the planes are the small Nazi ones that patrol Polish roads on lookout for guerrillas, Grandfather said.

"He can't leave the farm, because they watch him. We can stay on the farm, because they take our vegetables as soon as they are ready. Ours was a good farm. I am blind, so nobody minds me.

68

I came to Warsaw in a farmer's cart. I saw Stefan and he told me to come to you."

"We'll help you to get home, Michal," *Stryj* Franek said. "Don't go near the meadow again, and tell your grandfather to stick close to the farm. One night soon you will hear an owl call twice, then twice again. Turn out the lights then, but leave the door open."

The tall, thin man looked at the children gravely. "It may sometimes be difficult for you to understand how enemies turn into friends, for a time at least. But these are the politics and conveniences of great states, and Poland is only a small nation. We here all remember that when the Germans attacked Poland in September 1939, the Communists eagerly helped them and fought against us too. But now, as Jan knows and all of you must remember, since this past June 1941, the Russians have signed a pact with our Allies in the West, so we must help them however we feel in our hearts about their earlier treachery. If this airfield is indeed the one we in the underground have been trying to find, then it is of the greatest importance to put it out of action. It is difficult for us Poles to accept it, but accept it we must that when we help the Russians against the Germans, we are helping our Western Allies and bringing the day of liberation closer. We pray."

To the great chagrin of the boys, *Stryj* Franek refused to let them help.

"You have your own job to do," he said

sternly. "There are others who can deal with this. One day you may be captured, don't forget that, and then it is better for everyone if you know as little as possible about other operations."

But one evening, a week later, he came to see them.

"You deserve to know that everything went well," he said. "Your young friend Michal was of great help. It was a stormy, pitch-black night. We couldn't find our way, but Michal was our eyes. The darkness made no difference to him so he led us. There are no planes, buildings, or Germans there, and the runways are full of potholes. We did not lose a man. Grandfather and Michal are not suspected. And what a bang it was!"

Stryj Franek's tired face lit up with a smile.

"I hope you'll find a lot more friends like Michal."

After the excitement of helping to find the secret airfield, the daily work on the newspaper might have seemed a little dull to the small group of friends except for the fact that there was also their dangerous adventure of going to school.

 Stryj Franek had insisted on their attendance whenever possible. Jan and Stas had their advanced classes. Kazio went to an underground school only twice a week for there were not enough teachers left alive or outside of concentration camps to go around for all the children of Warsaw. Marja and Wanda went to the same teacher, though Wanda was two years older, and on those days, Kazio would take the little ones to the welfare center. Perhaps some milk had been brought in from the country for them, or an International Red Cross parcel had arrived.

The girls' school started at 2:10 p.m. one day; perhaps, at a quarter to four another day, for no underground meetings were ever held on the hour. For some reason, Nazis seemed more suspicious of people meeting on the hour, or at half-past than at irregular times.

"School day today, Marja," Wanda said one morning while feeding Pawel and the twins. "Do you remember how in the Other Days our mothers used to send us to school, neat and tidy? And schools used to start at eight in the morning instead of only 'when it's safe,' and school was always the same house? Now, it's flying school and we look like this."

Marja's wide gray eyes were suddenly full of tears. But Marja *never* cries, Stas found himself thinking. He jumped up from the table.

"Why don't we spruce up?" he demanded. "I'm going to get us a piece of soap!"

"Soap!" they laughed at him. "And why not needles and thread too!"

"And scissors, to cut our hair," Wanda added with a sigh.

"Start heating lots of hot water," Stas said. "Everybody shall have a bath. Kazio and I'll go shopping. Come on, my friend."

"A bath!" Wanda said. "Stas is silly, but

nice. Well, let's heat the water anyhow. Just perhaps they *will* find something."

"It's like having a real family, all of us being together," Marja said slowly. "Anyhow, we can rinse our clothes in the hot water and dry them in the sun. Lots of people haven't even hot water these days."

"And we have water from the well in the garden, and driftwood the boys gather on the river shore, and the sun is shining. Let's get out our wardrobe and see what we can manage."

While the water was boiling, they put out all their clothes. There was little beyond the things they wore. These were skimpy and ragged, because they'd had them since Poland was occupied, and the adults who had cared for them in the first months had disappeared or died.

"We really ought to make Pawel some shorts for the spring," Wanda said, "and the twins need tunics. But out of what? If we cut up a blanket, what will we use for a blanket?"

"The eaves in our loft," Marja cried. "There was a curtain left in one of the windows. I'll get it!"

Though faded, the old curtain was still whole, and of good strong cloth. They spread it out in the sun.

"In Other Days I just wanted to play or read," Wanda said thoughtfully. "Now I am glad when I find something useful to do. There's enough here for the twins' tunics too."

"The strangest thing, to me, is the freedom

we have," Marja said. "You know, no one to say 'you must come in now,' or 'go to bed,' or 'get up.' Sometimes, it makes me feel lonely."

"And a little afraid," Wanda said, looking curiously at Marja. Perhaps at last Marja would tell about her life before the occupation.

But just then Kazio jumped over the stone wall into the little garden. "Two needles!" he shouted. "And scissors. Only for lend. From Grandmother Zofia."

"Your own grandmother?" Wanda asked, surprised.

"Oh, no. She used to live on our street. She is so old everyone calls her Grandmother."

When Stas came back, he had two big pieces of soap.

"There is only one place where you could get soap like that," Wanda said, frightened. "From the Germans."

"Sure. It was quite simple. I know two boys who clean the washrooms in the German Officers Mess. Traitors, working for the Germans. I beat up one of them, took his coat and cap and walked right in there. Took the soap. Walked out again. Truly."

"You know you aren't supposed to take unnecessary risks."

"This was necessary," Stas said. "But mind you, I wouldn't like to do it every day."

"Let's not argue or worry," Marja cried. "We'll wash the little ones' clothes, the boys' shirts and our aprons first. Then we'll feel at least partly clean. There's lots of water. You wash the babies and yourselves, and Wanda and I'll wash the clothes."

They were all busy when Jan came home. He was carrying a bunch of flowers.

"We are going to have a feast!" he called. "*Stryj* Franek sent you some turnips, onions, a soup bone, and a bit of salt!"

"Oh, where did you get the flowers?" Marja asked.

"On the street where the new apartment houses used to be."

"Such a lot of flowers grow in the ruins!"

"You know why that is, don't you?" He saw how busy they all were. "What can I do while I tell you?"

"You can cut everyone's hair," Wanda said, taking the food from him. "Don't start the story until I've put the stew on."

So while the girls put the clothes to dry on the grass in the sun, and Jan started to cut Stas's newly washed hair, he told them.

"You probably won't remember, but in the days of peace the good mayor of Warsaw, brave Stefan Starzynski, asked all the Warsavians to plant flowers. 'I want to see my city green and full of flowers,' he said. Everybody liked him so well that they planted their gardens full of flowers, and people who lived in apartments had flower boxes at each window. Now those seeds and bulbs are coming out of the ruins again."

"What happened to the mayor?" Marja asked.

"He was falsely accused and put into a concentration camp," Jan said. "The Nazis hated him because they knew it had been his courage and bravery that made Warsaw hold out so long. The underground is still trying to find him. If he is alive, they'll rescue him, whatever the cost."

Together, they worked all morning. As the clothes dried, Marja sewed up the tears with thread Wanda pulled from the edge of the curtain. She even fixed patches across the seats of Kazio's and Pawel's trousers, for the washing had finally worn the material through.

By the time Jan got around to cutting the girls' hair, he was pretty good. Jadwika's and Ludwika's bangs were a little lopsided but he claimed they looked artistic. Marja washed her hair, but kept her pigtails. Wanda wanted her hair cut short, but Jan only trimmed it.

"We don't look particularly elegant," said Wanda doubtfully.

"But we do look a couple of shades lighter," Marja smiled. "And I am going to take those flowers to the teachers as in Other Days. May I, Jan?"

"Of course," Jan said, "but remember, if you meet any Germans you are not taking them to a *teacher!*"

The scent of lilacs drifted over the high fences of the old courtyards. They walked briskly.

When they came to a street of faded old rococo houses, Wanda glanced carelessly at the second floor window of the fourth house from the corner. The blind was halfway down.

As they passed the doorway of the fourth house a Gestapo guard, standing just inside, looked at them suspiciously. The girls didn't stop, neither did they hurry.

"Grandmother *will* be pleased with these flowers," Marja said loudly, though her voice shook a little. She kept up a cheerful-sounding chatter until they were out of earshot.

"We'll try school No. 2," Wanda whispered.

"Hear my dates," Marja begged. As they walked, she reviewed her history lesson, "King John Sobieski of Poland saved Europe from the Turks in 1683 . . ."

That kept their minds busy as they crossed a park to a street of apartment houses. Half of them were in ruins, but the sixth one from the corner had only had its top stories blown off. In the basement window was a pot of geraniums.

"There's the All Clear," Marja whispered. They ran down the steps and the shabby door opened as they reached it.

"The last door on the left," a girl their own age said.

In a small room, there were already some

forty children sitting on the floor, on boxes and packing cases. There was a makeshift blackboard on the far wall. Marja went up to the thin woman standing beside it.

"Flowers for the teacher." She curtsied.

A chuckle ran through the room. The teacher's eyes brightened.

"I am glad no one was caught at No. 1," she said. "We learned of the Nazi building inspection too late to warn you individually, but all of you have been very alert to the danger sign. Next week we'll meet at No. 4 if all is well."

A boy at the back of the room said softly, "That's why we say flying school."

The teacher smiled. "That's a good name for it. Well, let's continue. Instead of history, we'll have a lesson on current affairs today. Can anyone tell me about the present government of Poland?"

Wanda knew the answer. *Stryj* Franek had explained it to them. She stood up.

"The legal Polish Government operates from London today. Our active army, navy, and air force headquarters are also there. This government must answer for all its acts, to the Polish people, when we are free again."

A boy stood up: "While the Free Polish Government operates from London, they have representatives here, in Poland. My father is one of them. They make decisions about traitors, sabotage, schooling, everything, just as though Poland were free."

78

A boy next to him nudged him, and jumped up too: "My father works for the army. He is a captain. It is called the Underground Army because they have to maneuver and fight in secret, but it *is* the legal Polish Army, fighting against the Nazis, here in Poland. They get their instructions from the Polish Government in exile, in London, and from the representatives of the Polish Government here." He smiled at the boy next to him. "From *his* father, sometimes."

"That is correct," the teacher said. She spoke as though she were teaching them A B C, and she did not bother to tell them that what they had just said was dangerous if anyone who heard them was a traitor. She was aware that these children of Poland knew many secrets, in these dangerous years. If even one of them could be bought by a German Nazi she too would find herself in a concentration camp.

Then she said, "There is another branch of the Polish Government called 'Directorate of Civil Resistance.' Traveling by secret routes, and accepting danger, the representatives of our government and army keep in touch with one another, just as though the times were normal. They plan for the future of all of you, growing up to be proud Poles. We must obey their laws, and rules, just the way we would in times of peace."

The teacher discussed all aspects of Polish Government in wartime and peace. Then she said, "Professor Gorski cannot come to teach you mathematics today. Remember him in your prayers. The class is dismissed."

Four children got up. Two went out the way Wanda and Marja had come, two went out by the door at the back of the room. A few minutes later, another four got up to go.

"We can write about the government for the paper," Marja suggested, while they waited for their turn.

"We'll ask Jan," Wanda agreed.

They met the boys on their way home. Jan's face was shining. He looked a different boy when he was happy. He said, "I'm going to be able to try my *matura*, and perhaps take University level classes next year!"

"He has passed all the examinations," Stas said. "Imagine, he'll be only seventeen when he enters University. We have a brain trust in our midst!"

The reason we aren't any unhappier, Wanda thought as they walked companionably home, is because there is so much to do. Pawel wasn't looking well, and the twins were pale and thin, but then, suddenly, there was news that despite the difficulties, Jan had done well at his studies. It was a constant worry to find enough, or even almost enough food, for everybody, but the children's paper was doing well. And there was the danger of flying school, and patching and darning if one could find things to patch and darn with, but there was little time left over for worrying.

She hoped Kazio had found just something a bit different to put into the same old soup tonight.

A piece of spinach could balance the worry. Something good; so one could face the bad.

They'd get along.

10

One evening *Stryj* Franek slipped in through the kitchen door of the little house. He looked strained and weary. For the first time, he accepted Wanda's offer of a bowl of soup. Usually he would not eat with them because, Jan and Wanda realized, he did not want to deprive them of the little food they had.

Then he did another unusual thing. He told them about one of the adult underground printing shops that had been raided. Seven patriots had been captured, two shot, their supplies burned, their shop demolished.

Usually, he told them only what he wished

them to do. He had said to Jan, and Jan had told the others, that the less any of them knew of any other underground operation the better. Then they wouldn't have to try not to tell, or tell lies, or perhaps, ultimately—with German torture—tell all, if they were captured.

This was so unusual that Jan said, "Can we help?" The rest of the children crowded about him.

"Would you please," *Stryj* Franek said. "It's important. We have heard by radio, that today, during the London blitz, the Polish Air Force shot down twenty-seven German planes, bombed two factories in Germany, and sank one U-boat. It is heartening news to us at home, and it is better still if we can say it happened just yesterday. The pamphlet ought to be on the streets tomorrow. The sooner the people get the news, the stronger the propaganda value. It would show the Germans we don't believe their defeatist lies."

"If we work all night," Wanda said matter-of-factly, "we'll have to take the babies with us."

"Print in the front of the pamphlet 'How to Grow Parsley,'" *Stryj* Franek said. "I'll help you carry the twins to your office."

They were used to the dangerous night walk through the shadows and the ruins. They brought the rest of the soup and what bread they had left, and once in the cellar beneath the walls, they started to work. Every time they printed, "How to Grow Parsley," they laughed.

They worked through the night, and had

enough pamphlets ready for the boys and *Stryj* Franek to take out to distribute to the early workers. The girls continued to work the press, and the little ones slept. Stefan appeared at dawn; he always seemed to know when he was needed.

When Jan and Kazio came back for extra supplies, Jan said, "Funny, *everybody* wants to grow parsley today. We need help up there. When the noon crowds come out from the offices and factories, I think even the little ones could help. They'll be safe enough with all those people around."

"*Not* Pawel and the twins," Wanda cried. They didn't know the ages of the little ones for sure but the twins couldn't be more than six, and Pawel three. Even for distributing the children's paper, Wanda's rule had been that no one under eight could take on dangerous tasks.

"We do need their help," Stas said when he came down. "There was no time to get many of the others, and this has to be done fast."

"We'll give out the papers only in the center of the city, and then we'll be back," Jan said. So when Jan, Stas and Kazio took their next load of pamphlets up from the cellar one of the small ones went with each of them.

Wanda, Marja, and Stefan, tired and hungry, kept working as hard as before, but now the darkness seemed thicker, the press more loud, the creaking and groaning of the cellar passages more threatening. The moldy damp air made them cough; they glanced over their shoulders at shadows.

"I don't care what you think," Marja said after a time, still feeding paper into the press, "but I'm afraid. Pawel and the twins are too little."

In her heart, Wanda agreed completely. But she said, "They'll be back soon."

Stefan said nothing until they had used up all the paper they had. Then, abruptly, he began to dismantle the press.

"I don't like the feeling inside me," he said briefly. "People used to say my old grandmother was a witch, but it isn't that. I think we should move now. Anyhow the press needs cleaning and oiling."

He began to work frantically, unscrewing the type and the various parts. Marja brought him the two wicker baskets they used for carrying their supplies. They didn't question their sense of fear and urgency. They put all the things they kept in the cellar into the baskets. Wanda bundled up the pamphlets they had printed, and the proofs of the next number of the children's paper.

"I'm going to put these things behind the secret door, just for now," Stefan said.

Their emergency exit was a hole behind their makeshift shelves into the other flight of steps Jan had found during his first inspection. Stas had brought old boards and rubble they could push into it for camouflage, if they ever had to do so. The steps led through two basement passages to a

ruined house which had an arch on the other side
of the walls. They knew the way well. They'd prac-
ticed going out that way because Jan had said it
might be useful.

"Go ahead, though I don't think it's necessary." Wanda tried to sound comforting. "I'm
going to go up to the streets and find the little ones
now."

Right then, they heard a stumble and a
shuffle down the cellar steps. Marja caught Jadwika
before she fell.

"Q-quick," the little girl was crying, "Nazi
bad men. Coming here."

She burst into loud sobs and Wanda knelt
by her. "Pawel? Ludwika? Jan?"

"No time for that," Lame Stefan moved in-
credibly quickly. "Wanda, take the baby through.
Marja, catch hold of this basket."

Wanda pushed Jadwika through the emergency hole, and ran up the steps. Stefan and Marja
lifted the last of the baskets through. Then Stefan
went back and swept rubble from the corners of
the room, to cover their dusty footsteps before he
pulled the shelf back into place. Marja and he
threw down Stas's boards and rubble to cover the
exit.

When they got the baskets up the steps to
the basement above the underground cellar, Stefan's crutch fell. Already, in their office, she could
hear the Germans. But what could Stefan do with-

out his crutch! It wouldn't take them long to find the little trap door. She ran.

Up in the basement, a bald, short man was heaving their precious baskets to his shoulder. Jadwika was sobbing in Wanda's arms.

Stefan said, "It's all right. It's Bronek from the forest. He's got stables, near here."

Bronek's voice was rough. "You girls get home, right now. Out through the arch, down the slope beyond the walls, and home. The Nasties will be crawling through here like locusts in a minute. We'll try to save your press. Get going!"

It began to rain as they ran. They lost the way. Jadwika cried at the top of her voice. They tried to shush her, and she cried louder.

Finally, they couldn't remember how, they were home.

Automatically, Wanda put the pot with their last potatoes and an onion on to boil. Marja dried Jadwika with an old blanket. Rain slashed at the windows now.

For the first time in years, in front of anyone, Wanda sat down on the floor and cried. Marja hugged her.

"Stop it, stop it," she said. "I'm going to put our Sunday herring into the soup. It's beginning to smell anyhow. They'll be back."

"The Nazi bad men took them," Jadwika said clearly from her blanket nest. "They took everybody. But Kazio was mean. He rolled on the street and he pushed me, and he told me to go to you."

"Tell us, what happened?" Marja held the little girl close.

"There is no time for that now." Inside the kitchen door stood a tall man in a cloak fastened by a wide belt. He had an odd stocking cap on his head and his voice was husky. In a flash, Wanda remembered him. He was the strange man who had helped them the night the Nazis stole the Jan Kilinski statue and Kazio arrived.

"We must stay," Wanda said. "The boys will be coming back, *here*. They have nowhere else to go. And Pawel. And Ludwika."

"The Gestapo have nosed out this place. Hurry," the tall man said. "Upstairs. It's the only way now. The boys won't be coming."

As though he had always known the way, he carried Jadwika up the ladder to the loft. When Marja and Wanda had climbed up too, he pulled it up after them.

"As soon as the Germans are inside the house, out we go," he said. "There are only three of them."

This was precisely what *Stryj* Franek had told them to do in an emergency, Wanda remembered. Who was this man who knew the secrets of the little house!

The man was listening. They heard the kitchen door slam. They heard tramping through the rubble in the front of the house.

"Now!" The stranger slipped the ladder out of the loft window. It was screened on the outside by lilac bushes growing close to the house. They were drenched before they reached the ground.

"Past the ruins, over the far wall," the stranger whispered. He had Jadwika inside his cloak. She was quiet now.

They had worked all night and all morning. They were too tired to think. They stumbled after him through the gray, slashing rain. Wanda's dragging footsteps beat out the names of her friends, Jan-Stas, Pawel-Pawel, Kazio, Ludwika, Jan-Stas, on and on. She held out her hand and Marja gripped it tightly.

Finally, the man in the cloak said, "In here, young friends. Don't give up. You have many things to do. Be of good heart."

He pushed them through a door to a warm passage and into a little room rosy with firelight. A very small, old woman hurried to them, but for a moment they could not hear what she was saying. Pawel and Ludwika had hurled themselves at the girls.

The stranger who had helped them had slipped away.

11

It was a poor room but very tidy and cheerful with the fire and many plants in earthenware pots. The little old woman made the girls take off their wet clothes and drink mugs of hot broth before she let them talk at all.

"She's the Grandmother Zofia, Kazio's grandmother," Pawel kept saying.

"I'm a great-great-grandmother to many children." The old woman's smile was toothless but as friendly as her eyes.

"Jan, and Stas, and Kazio," Wanda said. "Please, what happened?"

"And how did Pawel and Ludwika get here?" Marja asked.

"Nice man in a funny hat brought us here," Pawel said.

Bluntly, the grandmother said, "The Germans caught the boys. Now, no grieving. That's wasted energy."

"I'm going to *Stryj* Franek." Wanda got up.

"You wait until your clothes are dry, and you've had another mug of good herb broth inside you. Rushing about like a headless hen will do none of us any good."

Marja said, "Ludwika, you tell us. Start from the beginning."

"We went with the big boys to the square with lots of people there," Ludwika said obligingly. "They gave away the little books, Jadwika too. Pawel and I sat on the extra sack, like Jan told us. One lady talked to me in funny Polish. She said, 'Would you like to be my little girl in Germany?' I said no, but she talked and talked. Then trucks came and Nazi bad men jumped out. The lady went to look at them and I took Pawel's hand because he was crying."

"My eyes hurt," Pawel said.

"Then the nice man came and picked up Pawel and me, and we saw Jan and Stas in a truck, but we didn't see Jadwika or Kazio."

"That's how Jadwika got away," Marja said slowly. "The German lady thought she'd been talk-

ing to *her* instead of Ludwika. So Kazio had time
to tell her to run and warn us."

"That strange man in a cloak is always there
when you need help." Wanda stared hard at
Grandmother Zofia. "Could he be Jan Kilinski
who fought for Poland a hundred and fifty years
ago! Could it be he?"

The old woman's eyes were hooded. "The
heroes of Poland have defended our people and
our land, always. Time means nothing to them.
They come when there is need of them. That's all
we need to know."

She soaked hard bread in the herb broth
and gave each of the small ones a plateful. Then
she said briskly, "But of course we must help ourselves also. God helps those who help themselves.
Come here, Wanda girl. This is an old district and
you can easily get lost in our jumble of streets and
alleys. I shall show you a safe way to go, and to
come back. If you are careful you will all be safe
here for a time."

Marja wanted to go too but they decided it
would be safer for Wanda to look for *Stryj* Franek
by herself. After all, he too might have been captured.

Night had come when she went out. She felt
fearful now, as on the night Jan had found her.
Again there was the uncertainty and great danger.
But she didn't feel as hopeless. Their months of
work together, and the refuge in the little house,
had given her confidence.

She didn't get all the way to *Stryj* Franek's hideout. Halfway there, he appeared from an alley and walked beside her. He was wearing his workingman's clothes but his voice was that of a stern professor.

"You must try to understand, Wanda," he said. "We cannot help you. The underground has suffered many losses. The Germans have taken dreadful revenge on innocent people. We cannot risk the lives of any others to save the boys."

"But Jan is your nephew!" Wanda cried.

"I cannot make an exception of him. He knew, *you all knew right from the beginning*, the risks you took. You knew the rules. We cannot endanger either the underground, or the people of Warsaw, for a few."

"You will do nothing?"

"I cannot." *Stryj* Franek's voice was grim. "Now, go to the end of this alley, turn right, you will find your way home. Go with God."

Now, when there was no one to see, Wanda cried. She sobbed as she stumbled through the darkness. She had been so sure *Stryj* Franek would be able to help. It had been dreadful when Bronislaw was shot, but she had never known Bronislaw. These were her friends: Jan, dark, tempestuous Jan who one day might have been another one of Poland's great musicians. Stas, so gay, and fair, and enterprising. Little Kazio with his red hair and clever hands. She huddled in a broken doorway and cried and cried.

93

"Wanda. Wanda, that is not the way."
After a time she heard the low voice. She wiped her
eyes and stared into the darkness and finally made
out the shape of the stranger in the cloak.

"You are Jan Kilinski, a ghost." Her voice
was hiccuppy with crying.

"It doesn't matter who I am. I am a Pole.
Dry your eyes, Wanda. You will not help matters
by crying. There are things to be done."

"The underground won't help," Wanda
swallowed, but she stood up.

"The paper must still come out on time.
That is your duty to Jan and to all the others who
have taken great risks." The stranger had his hand
lightly on Wanda's shoulder. "You are never alone,
fighting for Poland, remember that. We are a
goodly company. . . ."

"Wanda? I've been waiting for you." The
short, bald man, Bronek, ran toward them. Toward
her. Where had the tall stranger gone?

Ahead, she recognized the doorway of
Grandmother Zofia's house. Bronek was talking
fast, "I knew the underground wouldn't be able to
help. But don't get discouraged. There are other
ways. You are the oldest now; you'll have to take
the lead. I wanted to catch you before you go in.
The little ones are miserable in there. You'll have
to tell them there's hope. I've got the press, see.
Stefan and I have got it all set."

"I won't cry again," Wanda said.

"Don't forget the men from the forest,"
Bronek said. "And I have a plan."

94

12

Bronek explained his plan carefully.

"Haven't you heard about the forest guerrillas, Wanda?" he asked. "The Men of the Forest. We are not part of the regular underground nor of the government. We like to do things when we see something to be done, and fast. The underground can't be blamed for what we do, because even the Nazis recognize our different way of going into action. I'm their man in Warsaw, but I'll contact them, and fast."

He glared at Wanda and continued, "There's an excellent reason to save the boys; they are a symbol of the courage of the children of Poland. If they are saved, Polish children will feel their efforts are truly worthwhile.

"But you must keep on the job, my girl," he added. "That's what's expected of you and that's what you must do. You'll be hearing from me."

The bald, round-faced, little man gave Wanda an encouraging clap on the shoulder.

"Cheer up the others. Until tomorrow, then!"

Early the next morning, Stefan came to show them the way to Bronek's hideaway. Not a house had been left standing in this particular block. Homes of peaceful, happy people were now great mounds of stone and rubble. But Bronek had found a part of an old stone stable, strong enough to bear the weight of the wreckage above. It was a good headquarters for a man whose business was secret.

Bronek had raided a German office for paper and printing ink. Stefan had set up the press. There was an old door, with bricks for legs, as a table.

"I've put out a call for the rest of the gang," Stefan said, pleased with the girls' surprise. "You write, Bronek and I'll do the printing. We'll get the paper out right across Warsaw, just like always."

"Bronek, do the Nazis know who the boys are and what they've been doing?" Marja asked.

"Unfortunately, yes. They are very thorough."

96

"Then it won't do any harm to write their names?"

"They know them already," Bronek repeated.

"Write it, Marja," Wanda said. "That'll be front page. I've the proofs here for the rest of the paper."

Marja sat down by the makeshift table. Stefan handed her a pencil. I *must* do my very best, she thought. I *must* get this right.

She began to write:

Only yesterday Jan and Stas and Kazio were still running on the streets of our old Warsaw. They were like the rest of us, afraid and hungry. They were also courageous.

They started this paper you are reading today because they believed that all Polish children wanted to fight the Germans by never forgetting their proud heritage. Our best weapon against an enemy who wants us to grow up stupid is learning and knowledge. They want to make us into slaves, believing only what they say, working for them, and serving them.

Well, we aren't going to do it. We are going to learn and work for Poland, and we hope this little paper is going to remind us all to do just that.

It's going to come out just the way it did before Jan, and Stas, and Kazio were imprisoned by the Germans, the brave Nazis who make war against little boys like Kazio.

You can help by reading this paper, passing it on to your friends, and learning all you can.

She wrote on, of Jan's joy in music, of Stas's hopes of building a wonderful new Poland, of little Kazio's courage.

Under the story she drew the first notes of the "Polonaise."

Wanda, Stefan and Bronek read over her shoulder. Bronek gave a loud sniff, the only time his inscrutable front broke.

"Give me the first page," he said. "I'll start setting it."

For the next few days dozens of children ranged into every corner of Warsaw, handing out the little paper. The girls and Stefan, printing more papers each day, felt so hopeless they hardly talked to one another. Bronek had disappeared.

On the third day the Germans made one of their boastful errors.

They hung up posters with pictures of the three boys:

SOON THESE MISLED YOUTHS WILL TELL US
THE NAMES OF THEIR CONFEDERATES.

The message was printed in large letters in German and Polish.

THEY NOW KNOW WHAT IT MEANS TO TRY TO
STAND UP AGAINST THE GERMAN MIGHT.
NO ONE WHO DEFIES US REMAINS ALIVE FOR LONG.
THIS IS A WARNING TO ALL POLES.

That night Bronek came to Grandmother

Zofia's house where the children had been living since the night of their escape.

He looked tired, but he had a smile for them.

"The Men of the Forest have made their decision," he told them. "They will try to rescue the boys. I thought they would; whatever the risks there isn't a worthier cause for action. But the rest of you will have to hold yourselves ready to leave the moment I come to tell you, or send you a message. It won't be safe for you in Warsaw after this."

"What will we do until then, Bronek?" Wanda asked. To do nothing, just wait, would have been dreadful.

"Well, you could do one more thing. Paint as many posters as you have time and paper for. Just print this:

POLAND WILL LIVE WHILE HER CHILDREN
ARE VALIANT.

There'll be people to help plaster them all over Warsaw when the time comes."

He means *if* they can get the boys away, Wanda thought. The thought remained with her all the next day while she and Marja printed and painted the posters, and Stefan took the ready ones to his helpers in the secret caves in the ruins.

It was nearly midnight when he came hurrying back for the last time.

"Come quickly. Bronek will be fetching you from the grandmother's. Hurry now."

Grandmother Zofia had made a feast of bread, and broth, and potatoes. She had the little ones dressed. She had spent the days of their stay darning and patching their clothes.

Bronek came before dawn.

Stefan suddenly looked paler, thinner, more ill than ever before to Wanda. She hugged him. He bent to ruffle Pawel's hair. He pulled Jadwika's thumb out of her mouth.

"Come with us," Marja said.

"I must keep working here. Whenever you can, send the paper. We'll get it distributed. I wish I could write it, but I can't. I'm going to miss you."

"We'll see you again," Wanda said firmly. *"We will see you!"*

Stefan turned his back. Grandmother kissed them all, quickly. Bronek hurried them out of the little house. He picked up Pawel.

"We must get out of the city before morning," he said. "Hurry."

Moonlit Warsaw, though destroyed and unhappy, seemed lovely to Wanda this night. She had never left it before except for summer holidays by the Baltic Sea. Now they were on their way, she didn't know where, and she wondered whether she would ever see Warsaw again. She found herself thinking of her mother, and quickly she reached for Jadwika's hand, and whispered to Marja to keep to the shadows.

Long before they reached a house on the outskirts of the city, they had to carry the sleepy twins. Pawel was snoozing over Bronek's shoulder. The little ones were cold, and they were miserable.

"Now," Bronek said. "Wake up. The guard is changing. Cross the road, and stay in the ditch until the woods. I'll carry the small ones."

The ditch led them into a pine copse. Ahead was only the ragged darkness of trees. Behind them, the voices of the road patrol faded.

"Quickly," Bronek said, hurrying them on. "Just a little farther. There's a back road through the copse."

They were so weary that they never quite remembered again how they finally got into the old touring car, who had helped them, who had driven. They awakened when it was already light. The car had stopped, and a new driver slipped behind the wheel. On the back seat, Pawel, Jadwika, and Ludwika were asleep under some old coats. Bronek had fallen asleep on the floor of the car, with his arms still stretched out to see they wouldn't fall.

The new driver was tall and thin. All Poles were thin by now, so that wasn't extraordinary. This man's eyes were sunken and his cheekbones stood out, but he sounded so cheerful it might have been peacetime.

"We'll be there soon now," he said. "Here, have some dried apples. They might not taste like peaches, but they've vitamins. Listen, do you hear the song of Vistula? Pretty soon we'll see the river, and you can listen to her singing of the mountains where she started as a little stream, of all the little villages she passed, and of the ancient cities her waters know so well."

He began to whistle, and they could almost hear the song of the river. They drove through the last of the trees and there was a scattered, small village ahead. The River Vistula flowed like a green ribbon behind it. They stopped by a wharf with a few boats tied up. Moored farther out was a river barge.

A small boat pulled away from the barge. With a shock, they saw that the two men in it were Gestapo officers.

Their driver hailed the boat. Then he looked down at the horrified girls.

"Don't panic," he said quickly. "They are our men."

Bronek had awakened and helped the three little ones from the car. The two men in German uniforms shook hands with him.

"So these are the other kids," one of them said. "We got the boys just about in time. The Germans were so sure of themselves we had no trouble. We walked in, gave them the papers signed by the *gauleiter*, and walked out. Had to carry the boys, of course, but they'll be all right."

"You sign a good *gauleiter* signature, Jerzy," the other man in the Gestapo uniform said to the driver. "We were saluted all the way out."

The tall man who had driven the old touring car laughed. "You may have been the best character actor in all of Poland, but now you must admit I am the best forger. I have orders to go down the river with the barge. And you?"

"Bronek? Ready to leave? We are going back to the forest." He held the rowboat to the quay. "Get in, children. You'll find friends on board."

Bronek said, "The best of luck to you. Send us the children's paper from wherever you are. We'll get it to Stefan and see that it's distributed. You'll find the press is on board too. Go with God."

The motor of the barge was already rumbling when they started to climb aboard. Bronek and the Men of the Forest waved from the shore.

Jan, Stas and Kazio, trying to smile, held out their hands to pull up the little ones. The tall man who had been the last driver of the touring car helped the weary girls.

13

Wanda had forgotten there could be days like this. Long, lazy days in the sun with little to worry about. The river slipped by and the barge churned steadily upstream. Birch trees and willows lined the riverbanks. The flat northern plains turned into verdant hill country.

With spring weather, the storks had flown back from Egypt, and in every small village they passed, they could see families of them, standing on one leg, on top of a bare tree or on the roof gables. Many villagers placed old cartwheels as a base for their nests and welcomed the same storks back year after year like old friends.

The barge passed under wooden bridges with thatched-roofed wooden houses lining the riverside, and many cupolaed wooden churches standing on the hills above the village.

The girls and the little ones sat on the deck in the sun and the strain and horror slipped away with the gentle flow of the river. After sleeping most of the first two days and nights, Jan, and Stas, and Kazio joined them too. They did not speak of their experiences in prison, but little by little the blank look was fading from their eyes, and the grayness from their skin.

Jerzy, the tall, thin man who had brought them to the barge, would sit with them, playing his bagpipes.

"You must be a Goral from the Highlands," Marja said one day. "Only the Gorals play those tunes. You are not a guerrilla at all."

"And you must be from the Highlands yourself, little lady, to recognize the old tunes," Jerzy said. "But you must remember no one is quite what he seems, these days. A guerrilla is a soldier for Poland. He may be the clerk and the bookkeeper, the lawyer, teacher, doctor and farmer, he could be a fisherman, a newspaperman, or a messenger boy. And it's better he remains nameless and homeless until Poland is free again."

One day when the barge passed through a large town, Jerzy hurried the children down into the hold.

"No point in having people ask questions,"

he said. "The barges are very necessary to us. They are one of our safest methods of communication because they've got all the necessary Nazi permissions, passes, and safe conduct clearances. And do you know why? Soon after the occupation, we persuaded some Highlanders, farmers and barge captains, to go to the top Nazis in Warsaw and offer to supply them with choice delicacies from the mountains: bison meat, snow-cured hams, salmon and trout from the mountain streams, cheese, fowl. The Germans love their stomachs, and they were so happy to find some 'reasonable Poles' that now the safest way for the underground to move, or send messages, is by river barges. Neat, don't you think?"

But mostly, Jerzy would tell them tales of Poland's past. He'd point out hills topped with historic castles or the sites of ancient battles and tell them the legends and sing them the songs of lands they passed. The day Stas was showing Pawel how to draw an eagle—the emblem of Poland—Jerzy told them this legend:

"Once upon a time there were three brothers called Lech, Czech, and Russ. They lived in the primeval forests of Central Europe. One day, they decided to go their separate ways, exploring far lands. Lech went north. Over mountains, and through forests, and across marshes, he explored until he came to a fertile plain by a river.

"Here he found a nest of a white eaglet. Since eagles' nests are mostly found only in high mountains, Lech and his followers thought this must be a very good omen, and they decided to stop and live there forever. And that," said Jerzy, "was the beginning of the town of Gniezno, which means 'nest,' and forever after the emblem of Poland was a white eagle."

"What happened to Czech and Russ?" asked the twins.

"Czech crossed the mountains to the southwest and settled in the lands that are now Czechoslovakia. Russ walked the fastest, on and on eastward to what now is Russia. And the story means, little twins, that the Poles, the Czechs, and the Russians all come from the same Slavic family and perhaps will one day live in peace together again."

"Could we still understand their language?" Stas asked.

"Yes, quite well. Many of our words are the same. The Czechs across the Tatra Mountains, in particular, speak much like us."

When they were getting close to the ancient city of Krakow, Jerzy told them of Krakus who lived in his wooden castle on the cliffs above the Vistula in prehistoric times. The people were terrorized by a dragon who lived in the caves below the cliffs and ate up Krakus's warriors and his cattle. His hide was so thick no weapon could pierce it so Krakus thought up a clever idea. He stuffed the skin of a sheep with sulphur and left it by the mouth of the dragon's cave. The greedy beast rushed out and swallowed it whole. Then the sulphur began to burn his insides. He crawled down to the river and drank, and drank, and drank—until he burst!

"Don't laugh," Jerzy ended the story. "I can show you the proof. There is a high mound above Krakow that Krakus's grateful people built for him, and that's how he became the founder of the city."

"It could be just a natural hill," Kazio suggested.

"It isn't," Jerzy said. "In ancient times, when Poles wanted to honor their heroes, they built them mounds. They built a mound for Krakus's daughter too. Her name was Wanda and she was almost as beautiful as our Wanda."

Wanda blushed, and the twins said, "Tell us about Wanda."

"She was beautiful and wise and the country prospered under her rule. A German prince decided he'd marry her and get all the rich lands. But Wanda didn't want a foreigner to rule her people. So the German prince threatened to invade Krakow if Wanda wouldn't marry him. But Wanda didn't want war either, so to solve the problem and keep her people free and at peace, she jumped into the Vistula."

The twins' lips began to tremble. Quickly, Jerzy said, "And all through the ages when somebody is very patriotic and brave, Poles still say that he, or she, is like Wanda. Isn't that a nice way to be remembered?"

But the stories all of them liked best were those Jerzy told them of the Tatra Mountains, and of the knights of Poland who are said to sleep in a great cavern under the mountains awaiting a call from King Boleslas the Valiant. They are the heroes who had died throughout the centuries fighting for Poland's freedom and independence.

"Boleslas lived in the year 1,000 and was the first crowned King of Poland," Jerzy said. "His body lies in the vault of the Wavel Cathedral in Krakow with all the other Kings of Poland.

"All through the year, the vault is dark and silent, but on Christmas Eve, if you listen, there rings the sound of clanging armor, strong voices, and swords striking in the caverns below. A bearded giant sits at the head of a huge, oaken table holding court. All the knights awaken in their mountains that night and come to Boleslas. 'Has the hour struck to free Poland?' they ask him. 'Not yet,' he says. And they return to their caverns in the Tatras again."

"Why doesn't he tell them to fight, *now?*" Kazio demanded.

"Perhaps he must wait for the right moment," Jerzy said sadly.

"We should write all these stories in our paper," Marja suggested.

Jan jumped up. "All except the one about Boleslas. That we'll save for the Christmas number. Let's get to work."

Just as he'd promised, Bronek had brought their press to the barge. Now that they were beginning to feel better, they started working on the paper again; which was a good thing because several nights later a motorboat pulled out of a village wharf they were passing and drew up to the barge.

The two men in it hailed Jerzy, and after a brief whispered conversation they spoke to the children.

"Stefan of Warsaw sends you his regards," one of them said. "He says all is going well, but he'd like some papers to distribute. In fact, if you can manage to make some extra copies for children in other towns, we will drop them off en route."

That made them work with renewed energy. But Jan also had a new worry. Where were they going, where could they live, how was he going to take care of all of them here in southern Poland where he didn't know anyone? The Germans couldn't keep check on every orphan child of Poland, but if a group was seen wandering aimlessly about they'd surely be picked up. He and Stas were big enough now for the Germans to send to their labor camps, and the same thing could happen to Wanda and Marja. What would the little ones do then?

"I don't know how I ever got myself such a large family," he said to Jerzy one evening. "I suppose it's not safe to stay in Krakow?"

"It would be very dangerous indeed," Jerzy said. "The Germans didn't bomb our old town, so they have made it the seat of their so-called government. They've taken it over like warrior ants. I've been longing to show Krakow to all of you because it's my town, and I think it's the most beautiful in all the world."

"But Warsaw of course is the most beautiful," Wanda and Stas said, laughing. Like everybody, everywhere, they thought their own city the best.

The day before they were going to slip by Krakow with the barge lights dimmed, Marja had a long conversation with Jerzy. Then he called Jan, Stas, Wanda, and Kazio to the stern of the boat.

"As I've told you," he said, "I'll have to leave you soon, to continue with my job. Marja hasn't told you that she thinks she knows of a place where you could stay, for a time at least, because she didn't want to raise your hopes in case it wasn't safe after all. But I know that it's still all right. You'll have to be just as careful as always, of course, but I think it's better than the hut in the mountains I had been thinking about for you. We'll drop you at dawn, several kilometers upriver from Krakow."

While they broke up the press again and packed their few things, they tried to question Marja.

"Let's wait and see," she said. "I'm still a little afraid. But if Jerzy says it's all right, there's at least a garden where we can plant things."

At dawn Jerzy woke the children.

"The skipper says we must leave you here. I am going to walk back to Krakow, where I have messages to deliver. His barge will be thoroughly investigated by the Germans farther up the river, so be sure you leave nothing behind. Marja will take you on from here."

He rowed them to the shore. Under a tall, gray-trunked weeping willow, he picked up Pawel. His face was sad, but he made his voice cheerful.

"I'll try to get some proper food for the little ones, though there isn't much hope. The Germans have plucked our poor country clean. My poor little Pawel."

Wanda wondered what he meant; then Jerzy was hugging her and Marja, shaking the boys' hands, lifting up the twins, and rowing back to the barge. She forgot about it. But she would remember it later.

They stood there for a long moment, watching the rowboat and the barge fade into the river mists of the early morning.

Then Jan said abruptly, for, after all, he had been the leader of the little group, "What did Jerzy mean, Marja? That you would show us the way?"

"Come with me. I used to live near here." She looked ready to cry. She had never told anything about herself, Wanda remembered. Perhaps she had never meant to. What had Jerzy said? That she didn't even know if her own home was still there!

They followed a path by the river. When the sun came up they gave the little ones bread and the fresh, fried fish the skipper of the barge had left them. The twins and Pawel, happy outdoors, became more lively than they had been in months. They ran about, picking flowers and stones, but they tired so easily Wanda wondered what was the matter with them. Of course she felt tired too, but then she was always hungry.

Half an hour later, Marja led them down a sloping hillside. Through the trees, in an overgrown park, they could see the towers of a castle. By broken stone gates, at the beginning of a wide grass-grown road, was a small thatched cottage.

"Come," Marja said, "we are almost there now."

A bent old man came limping out of the low house.

Marja walked slowly toward him. And then, suddenly, stumbling but fast, the old man ran to them. He bent on one knee and he took Marja's hands into his.

"Little Princess Marja." They could see he was trying not to cry. "You are alive! You are home again!"

14

"That's certainly some story," Kazio said, his freckled face and gap-toothed grin joyful. "Think of me knowing a real princess!"

They were sitting on a bench outside Old Wit's small cottage. His wife was calling loudly, as deaf people do, that the soup would be ready soon. It was a comforting, happy sound.

"Tell us everything from the beginning, please, Marja," Wanda begged. So, at long last, they heard Marja's story.

Her father was Prince Kazimir Poznianski, whose ancestors had lived in the castle they glimpsed through the trees for hundreds of years.

Marja's mother died when she was born, so when Germany invaded Poland and Prince Kazimir left to join his regiment in Warsaw, he took his little daughter with him. She hadn't heard from him since the day his cavalry regiment rode gallantly but pointlessly against the German tanks.

Her great-aunt's house, where she had been staying in Warsaw, was bombed. Marja had been dug out of the ruins, but her old aunt was buried in the rubble. She was taken to a welfare center where she met the twins. She had looked after them because everybody else was too busy.

When the Germans decided to send all children who looked Nordic to Germany to be brought up as Nazis, blond Marja realized both her danger and the fact that the small, dark, Jewish Jadwika and Ludwika would be sent to a concentration camp.

"Then I met you and practically made you take us in because I was really feeling desperate," she said. "When I saw Jerzy was bringing us near home, I told him that if Wit was still alive we'd be all right with him."

"Why didn't you tell us all this before?"

"It made me too sad," Marja said briefly. "And as for coming here, I didn't want to build up your hopes. I thought the castle surely would be occupied by the Germans. Why isn't it, Wit?"

The old man rubbed his hands and chuckled, "Old Wit used his head."

"I've never been in a castle," Kazio said. "Could we go, now?"

So, while the stew was cooking, the children walked up the long grass-grown drive, and Wit, very pleased with himself, explained what had happened.

"The Germans came down from Krakow in their cars. I stopped them at the gate and told them this was the private property of Prince Poznianski, but they pushed me inside and went on in. I got old Sigismund from the village and we made a plan. In a week, all the high and mighty German officers were rushing away in their cars, faster than they came."

"But why, Wit? What happened!" Marja cried.

The old man was shaking with chuckles. "The castle was haunted, little Princess! That's what happened."

"Why, Wit, you know that isn't true," Marja said indignantly.

"The castle was truly haunted, my Princess, by Old Wit, and Sigismund and Old Wit's wife. Oh, the Germans themselves heard the sad ghosts walking on the stairs, rattling their chains, sighing and groaning. Chairs vanished behind their drunken backs, glasses jumped on the table, drafts blew in closed rooms, and candles never stayed lit. It was most uncomfortable for the high and mighty Nazis."

"What did you *do*, Wit?" Marja demanded.

116

Wit spoke with mock penitence. "You know the old entrance? And the secret stair behind the library wall? And the panel in the dining room? The room in the tower you enter through the chimney? Well . . ."

"Oh, Wit! Pretending to be ghosts!"

"Well, it drove the Nazis away, didn't it?" The old man was pleased with the children's laughter. Then he sighed, "But they packed most of the furniture, paintings, silver, and plates and took them away. We hadn't time to hide more than a few little things, the defeat came so soon."

Marja took the old man's hand. "Never mind, Wit, I know you did your best. When Poland is free again, we'll get new things."

Wit had been right. The high, handsome rooms, the magnificent stairways, were empty. Tapestries had been torn from the walls, chandeliers pulled out, pictures cut from their frames. Dust and cobwebs covered the empty rooms. Only a small, paneled music room in the tower was almost as it had been. Perhaps in their rush to leave they hadn't known how to get the grand piano out through the window.

"Oh, Jan," Wanda said when she saw the piano, "play for us."

Jan stood straight and pale, his fists clenched. "No. These are not times for music. But," he added less fiercely, "we could use the castle for our workshop. Only we'll do the same thing as in Warsaw. We'll leave the dust and the cobwebs as they are in the front, and we'll find a room somewhere in the back for ourselves. It'll be safer."

After investigating thoroughly, they chose the old kitchen and servants' quarters to use as a workshop, and for their bedrooms in the summer. In the winter, as Wit pointed out, it would not only be impossible to heat such a huge drafty old place, but smoke rising from the chimneys of a supposedly deserted castle would certainly make some passing German suspicious. The loft in Wit's small cottage could be divided into two dormitories for the boys and the girls.

So they were all set with shelter and a workshop, but food was as great a problem here in southern Poland as it had been in Warsaw. The Germans had stolen all the crops; the farmers had nothing to sow. They had taken the livestock and the chickens. There was no longer either wheat or rye to make pure bread so everyone in the countryside mixed ground lupin seed and chestnut flour into the bread dough. There was fish in the river though, Wit said optimistically, and his wife used herbs and greens in her soups.

"I had better go to Krakow tomorrow," Jan said, "and consult with Jerzy. He promised to get our press off the barge, and perhaps he could find us some sugar and milk for the little ones."

"And when high summer comes, Old Wit's wife knows of a wild beehive in a forest meadow," said the old man happily.

Jan left at dawn, for it was some four hours'

walk to Krakow. It was lovely in the open country with the blue line of mountains to the south and the rich green of spring in the trees. Nothing could spoil the beauty of Poland, he thought, as he walked, whistling, until he saw the towers of Krakow from a crest of a hill.

After that, he made his way carefully, avoiding the roads and consulting the map Jerzy had drawn for him. He fought down the temptation to go and look at the old city. The Germans had set up their government there and many had brought their families, away from the threat of Allied bombers, to enjoy the Polish Highland spring. That was another reason there was no food for the Poles.

When Jan found the old stone house Jerzy had *not* marked on the map, the door was opened by a thin girl, almost as tall as Jan, with clever, brown eyes and thick, straight, brown hair. Jerzy appeared behind her.

"This is my daughter, Zosia," he said. "I hope you will let her help you. She is sure you could work up good circulation for your paper in Krakow as well, and I have a surprise for you!"

From somewhere, he had magicked a bigger, better press than they had had. It would be brought to the castle that night, he promised.

"It's better," he advised Jan, "that as few strangers as possible come to Wit's or the castle. You and Stas will have to deliver your bundles of the paper at a point by the river which I'll show you. From there, we will send them onward."

"We'll write a Krakow edition first," Jan suggested, "and tell the children and young people here what we have done in Warsaw. Could Zosia come back with me to tell us things about your city?"

While he hadn't been able to get any extra food for the small children, they now had paper, printing ink, and a press again. Zosia turned out to be a wonderful addition to their little group. Everybody liked her; she had a knack for writing, and with her knowledge of Krakow, they felt they were wonderfully well organized.

So they spent the summer. And even though all of them were getting thinner and tiring more easily, their hearts were high.

15

Autumn came so soon it surprised them. One evening when the yellow leaves of the birch and linden trees blew in the cool wind through the castle park Jerzy came to tell them he had made plans for their education.

After that, the pattern of their days changed. Twice a week Jan walked to the underground university in Krakow. They were never the same days, and never in the same place, but the classes were kept as regularly as possible. Teachers would come from the city and the villages to set problems and lessons for the others. Not only Wanda, Marja, Stas, Kazio and Zosia attended these lessons, but also a dozen children from the village below the castle. Pawel and the twins, and a few children of their age, were taught by the bigger ones in turn. They knew that education was as good a form of resistance as fighting. Poland would need them when the world was free again.

One day when Jan was leaving for his lectures, Wanda said, "Why, dear Jan, just *why* don't you ask for music lessons as well? You know you meant to become a pianist, in the Other Days."

The sullen look came over Jan's face. "Poland needs fighters, not musicians," he said. "I'll see you in the evening."

That day, the others had no lessons. They were going to their workshop in the castle to write articles for the next paper. The little ones were off with Old Wit's wife to a farm. She had heard there might be a goat there—with milk.

As they walked through the trees to the castle (they never used the main walk, so that a path would not be made by their feet, to show someone that people still lived in the castle), Stas said to the girls, and Kazio, "Jan ought to play. It would be better for him. Our families used to be friends, which is the reason we got together when we had no more families. I'll tell you what happened. It was a few days after the Nazis took over Warsaw. He was still practicing with his teacher, Miss Weisman. She was quite famous, and the Germans came in and arrested her because she was Jewish. They just took her. He was only a small boy then, and they left him. He hasn't wanted to play ever since. I think he is bursting with unplayed music and that's the reason he sometimes gets so angry."

"There's Kazio too," Wanda said.

"What about me?"

"If we ever get anything extra, we always give it to the little ones. You have as much need for food as Jan has need for music. But we think of you as big."

"That doesn't matter," Kazio said. "I didn't have that much when I was growing up. Now I have more. I know who Chopin is."

They worked all the long afternoon, talking, trying to remember things, and then the storm broke. It came as autumn storms do in the foothills of the mountains, with a roar and a slashing of sharp rain.

And with the storm, Old Wit came running, drenched, to the back door which they used.

"Nazis!" he shouted. "Hide. The babies are in the loft. You hide! Quickly, quickly, quickly!"

They could hear the roar of a heavy car coming up the soft grass-grown driveway. Thunder roared and lightning slapped arrows through the windows. The kitchen was full of their things.

"There is no time," Wanda said. "We'll just have to leave everything. Marja, Wit, where is the secret passage you told us about the first day we came?"

"We must save something!" Stas shouted. "I will fight. I will fight by myself, alone!"

"Bring the papers then, the ones we have printed."

Wit said, "Here, little lady, through the chimney. The staircase goes up to the tower."

They went through the chimney and into the tower, and there Marja opened a panel and they saw the music room beyond it. Dust was heavy there too.

"Don't go in," Stas said. "If the dust is undisturbed, they will perhaps not search further."

"What about Jan?" Wanda said. "He's coming home just about now. Shouldn't we go to warn him?"

Old Wit had vanished. Stas stood over the girls, suddenly looking older, and thinner, and terribly serious.

"You are staying here," he ordered. "I'll do what must be done."

And then, like a miracle, they heard the car go away. After what seemed a long time, Wit limped up the stairs and said, "The Nasties took one look at the dust and the cobwebs, and felt the freezing uninhabited air of our old castle. They were more comfortable in their car."

But the fear of the unexplained visit remained with the young people.

They did not feel like leaving the music room in the tower. They huddled there, speechless, afraid. Too many things had happened too often. Now, at last, they felt it was the end.

That was where Jan found them.

"I was nearly home when I heard their car," he said matter-of-factly. "I hid in the ditch. I stopped at Old Wit's. He told me they had said they had heard of a haunted castle and just wanted to have a look. Of course it looks awfully haunted with all the dust and cobwebs in the front. So what with the weather and everything, they went away."

He looked at his friends. For the first time, perhaps, he saw how much younger they were. Two, or three, or four years younger than he was. He felt their fear, and in his heart, he felt their dependence on him, just because he *was* that little bit older.

He said, "Let's see if this old piano goes. I brought back some potatoes, and Old Wit's kindly wife is making a soup. It'll take half an hour of cooking at least. Shall I play for you?"

Slowly Jan walked to the piano.

The keys were dusty, but in the dry mountain air, the strings hadn't lost their pitch. He looked for a stool, and with a familiar, loving touch, he bent over the keyboard.

He played very softly at first, remembering, concentrating so hard he did not realize Old Wit and his wife brought the small ones, blankets wrapped around them, into the tower room too. As he played, he told of how Chopin, when he realized he was dying in exile in France, asked that his heart be brought back to Poland, and a goblet filled with the earth of his homeland be buried with him in the foreign soil. So it was done and his heart is still in a church in Warsaw, while with his body in a Paris churchyard there is Polish earth.

While the storm blew north and the night came into the tower room, he played for his friends the music that had been written out of love of Poland. Pawel nodded close to Wanda. Marja and the twins were wrapped in an old curtain. Stas stared out of the window. Kazio sat close to the piano, suddenly understanding music. Old Wit and his wife brought in cups of hot broth. It cooled while everyone listened to Jan playing, at last.

Stas remembered the windy autumn day his father had taken him to look at the bridge he was building over the Vistula. His mother had called them "my engineers," and protested when they walked along the girders high above the slow, green river. There had been speeding clouds and bright sun and far below, by the marshy shores, herons flowing on their steady slow wings. The two of them, he and his father, had talked of the many things they would build, together.

And as the music flowed on, Wanda could almost smell the Baltic winds, heavy with pine, and salt, and freshness. There would be white breakers on the granite rocks of the Baltic, smoke making a sign from a ship, white gulls flying, and a family picnic by the northern sea.

Kazio, suddenly, in his memory, smelled the wonderful, strong leather tang of his father's shop. He saw the strip of sunlight coming through the low window and heard the little bell that rang when customers came in. He heard his father's deep, friendly voice and felt proud and happy. And, when he took his shoes off in the spring, he would not step on the small purple flowers in between the cobblestones, but he didn't know why he remembered all this in Jan's music.

To little Pawel there came a memory of someone he had loved well, who had loved him. He crept closer to Wanda. Then he slept lightly and dreamed he was running down a grass-grown hill; there were white flowers, and his legs did not feel tired at all.

The twins had curled up next to Marja. There were smiles on their faces and their warm, dirty, small hands were open as though, in their sleep, they were giving a present to someone.

Marja thought of the summer mountains and her father's tall figure ahead on the path, and the way he looked over his shoulder with a smile to encourage her. Marmots whistled in the Tatra Mountains, and the wind sang a song it never knew on the plains or in the valleys below. All around and below them were range after range of blue heights and far, far below, the bent ribbon of bright silver that was the River Vistula in the sun. By evening, they would reach a chalet, far in the peaks, and everyone would greet her father with affection because they had known him since he was as young as she was now. They would sit outside and watch the sunset and he would suck his pipe and speak of his father, and his father's father, and all the generations before—their own people—and how they had loved Poland and fought for Poland's freedom without a thought for themselves.

Jan played on. He was trying to give comfort to his friends. He was trying to tell them in music, better than in words, that their work, and fears, and hunger were worthwhile. He was playing to tell them that everything was worthwhile.

As he played, he began to understand all these things better himself.

16

Then, almost overnight, it was winter.

They were cold in the castle now, but they still worked there. It was safer for everyone, including good Wit and his wife, should there be a sudden inspection.

"Do you remember the day we met you and the twins in Saxon Park, and Jan was so furious because you sang silly words to a Chopin tune?" Stas stopped turning the crank of the printing press and laughed.

"What made you think of it?" Marja put down her pen. They were working on the Christmas number of the children's paper.

"I don't know," Stas said. "I just think we are so grown-up now. We've changed."

"That's true," Kazio said. "I've changed. I think of other people before I play tricks. And I know who Chopin is. And I can read."

"Do you ever remember how life used to be?" Marja said slowly. "Do you remember when there were too many bedclothes in your bed and you were too warm? And you had eggs, and fruit, and enough milk for breakfast?"

"I like this life," Kazio said. "I have more things to do. And I wouldn't ever have done anything like this, or known all of you, in the Other Days."

"We'll try to make everything better for everybody when Poland is free again," Jan said, his face flushed.

"It's quite strange how we came together," Wanda said. "Pawel and I because you forgot to be careful and whistled the 'Polonaise.' Then Kazio came because he was unhappy, and Marja and the twins sang the 'Polonaise' too. It isn't a *bad* thing, Jan, to sing words to a tune. It makes us feel we are all together."

Jan rubbed his forehead. "Yes, perhaps you are right. After all, it is almost a password now even though the Germans forbid the tune. Let's make Christmas words for the 'Polonaise.' "

They were busy trying out ideas when Zosia ran into the room. It had been her turn to give lessons to the little ones in Wit's cottage where it was warmer.

"Pawel is in awful pain! He's crying and crying."

"I'll come." Wanda jumped up. "He hasn't been acting like himself at all lately."

"We must get a doctor," Jan said grimly, "but where?"

"My father," Zosia was crying, "he is a doctor."

"Jerzy?"

"Yes. Truly."

"Stas, come! We'll try to find him."

"Jan, we *must* get the paper ready." All Wanda wanted was to go to Pawel and get a doctor but discipline had become part of her life. "Jerzy said there will be a pickup tonight. The paper will be the only Christmas present most Polish children will have."

For a moment, Jan looked fierce. Then he said, "You are right. Kazio must be the one to go."

They watched him from the window, through the frosty glass. He seemed such a very small boy in his skimpy jacket, patched, tight trousers, and worn, peaked cap pulled over his ears as he ran down the drive through the gently falling snow of the December evening.

"This story needs editing, Jan." Wanda pushed the sheets of paper across to the frowning boy. "I'll be back when I've seen Pawel."

Stas continued to set type. Marja bent her

head over her papers. She wanted to run to Wit's cottage too, hug the little boy, cry a little. After all, it had been Pawel who had found her and the twins, and in a way, brought her home again. She forced herself to think what she must write.

And the paper *was* ready when the two anonymous Men of the Forest knocked on Wit's door. They had carried the stacked sacks down from the castle, and Jan and Stas helped to load them into the sleigh.

"It's a specially large edition," Jan explained. "For Christmas."

"Fine," one of the forest guerrillas said. "They'll be welcome in Warsaw. This is a bitter winter up there. And I have a message for you. The lame boy wants to know if he can come here. The Nazis are on to him. We'll manage to get him here if you have room."

"Tell him he is welcome," Jan said grimly. "Tell him that."

"He says he has someone to carry on in his place." Then, unexpectedly, he took off his fur cap and shook hands with them all. "God keep you this Christmastime, young patriots," he said.

They watched the sleigh, runners screeching through the powdery snow, until they could see it no longer. Now they must wait for Kazio and Dr. Jerzy, if Kazio had found him. Pawel had cried himself to sleep as close to the stove as they could get him.

Moonlight was patterning the snow when

Stas called them to the doorway. They saw a tall, dark shape with a humped back moving tiredly on skis toward them.

"This is like old times! Getting a doctor out in the middle of the night." The words reached them before they could be frightened of the apparition. "Jan, rub Kazio's nose with snow. It looks frozen. It was a long brave trip for a little lad."

Stas helped him out of his heavy workman's coat. His face in the firelight was tired and thin as he bent down to examine little Pawel.

"I have been afraid this might happen," he said finally, his voice sad. "It is happening all over Poland. There are many children like Pawel today."

"What is it?" Wanda whispered.

"Scurvy," Dr. Jerzy said. "It was the dread disease of the olden times, but in our modern days, we'd practically forgotten it. It is caused by lack of vitamin C, that is, lack of oranges and lemons, milk, butter, green vegetables. Scurvy is very painful, and can hit you suddenly like this. There is bleeding between the bones and the covering membrane and that's why Pawel, for example, holds his leg and wrist as though they were paralyzed."

"Where does one get milk and butter when there's hardly a cow left in all of Poland except for German use," Jan said bitterly, "and even in summer, they confiscated our crops of vegetables before they were barely ripe and sent them to Germany."

Wanda said, "Will he—will he—"

"Yes, Wanda," Dr. Jerzy said gravely. "He will die if he doesn't get proper foods. And where, *where* in all Poland can we get that today!"

"What would save him?" Jan asked.

"Simple things in a world at peace, but impossible to find in Poland," Dr. Jerzy sighed. "If we could get vitamins, concentrated cod liver oil, powdered milk, powdered eggs, if we could just get a reasonable amount, we could help a number of children."

"And if we don't?"

"I cannot work miracles." The tall doctor stood in the shadows, and his voice was full of pain.

Next morning, Jan looked as though he hadn't slept at all.

He came to Wanda who was cooking their thin breakfast broth on the stove.

"I can't just sit here and watch Pawel die," he said. "I'm going to try to get help.

"It can be done," his words stumbled over one another. "Others have made their way to England. I can do it too. I thought of it all night. The Czech border isn't far. Then I'd cross through Hungary to Yugoslavia. Remember the underground report about British ships bringing supplies and weapons to the patriot soldiers hiding in the Serbian hills? I could try to contact them. They might give us some of the foods we need, or I could get to England on one of those ships."

"Jan!" Wanda said, but Jan talked on.

134

"Once in England, I could see the members of our government. I could talk to the other Allies. You remember the story *Stryj* Franek sent us about how they are planning to help us by setting up the United Nations Relief and Rehabilitation Administration? At least, I must try."

"What about your job here, Jan?" It was Dr. Jerzy. "I couldn't help hearing you. You were shouting."

"The paper is going well. Stefan is coming down and he will help. Even Kazio is now writing some of our stories. Zosia is splendid. They can do without me. There would be more food, too, without me. And I am old enough now to join the Polish Air Force, and perhaps, even be able to help drop packages of supplies for children. Here, anytime, I could be caught and sent to a Nazi slave-labor camp."

"You have an answer for everything." Dr. Jerzy smiled.

"I ought to have." Jan found an answering grin. "I was up all night thinking, and I can't, I simply can't sit and do nothing for Pawel."

Everybody had gathered to listen by now. Stas said, "I'll come too."

"Two boys of your size on the road would make the trip doubly dangerous," Dr. Jerzy said. "No, I don't think that would be wise."

"Even one boy alone would look suspicious," Wanda said quickly. "But a boy and a girl might just be going for a walk, might they not?"

"You can't go if I can't go!" Stas shouted.

"It's an idea." Dr. Jerzy nodded thoughtfully. "At least one of you could have a chance to get through."

"We'll manage." Marja's face was full of sadness and disappointment, but she tried to sound cheerful. "Any minute now even the twins will be writing stories."

"The first thing you must do is to get permission to travel from the underground," Dr. Jerzy said. "I'll go to Krakow and contact the necessary officials."

Everyone who worked for the Polish underground, including children, was considered directly under the orders of the Polish Underground Government. The Nazis might think they'd defeated Poland, but the Poles had never stopped fighting in their hearts, and a risk to one was a risk to all. To help one was to help all.

Only Pawel did not feel the change that seemed to fall upon their days as soon as it was decided Jan and Wanda would go. They felt their young private fortress against the world was breaking up. Perhaps, after all, he too felt it, because, feverish though still sweet-tempered, he would beg for the story of King Boleslas to be told him again and again.

"I want to go to tell him to ask his knights to fight, when they come to see him at Christmas," he'd say. "Please, Wanda, may I go?"

"Not this year, Pawel dear," Wanda replied.

He was feverish and weepy on the afternoon of Christmas Eve. The other children had gone to fetch a Christmas tree from the woods, and the boys wanted to check their traps in case by lucky chance they'd caught a hare. Even wildlife was rare now, after three years of constant hunting.

Wit's old wife, who rarely spoke, suddenly said, "Why don't you go to the cathedral, my girl? Perhaps the child is right. Perhaps the old King needs to be told again we have need of his help. I'll look after him."

So Wanda got into her shawl, and coat, and the boots Wit and Kazio had made for all of them from old rugs left in the castle. It would be a long walk to Krakow, but, she thought, it would be much longer to the Adriatic coast of Yugoslavia. And in her heart, she knew she wasn't going for Pawel alone. She wanted to go for herself. They'd always gone to church this night.

Immediately, she had luck. Near the village below the castle, she got a lift with a farmer going to visit his family in the city. His horse was too old for the Germans to have "liberated," and the sleigh was warm with straw.

Wavel Hill was barricaded, the farmer warned Wanda, long since the Nazis had stolen the art treasures of the castle and the cathedral, but they still kept guard over the ancient buildings.

But she had promised Pawel. In her heart, she had promised herself too. It was a risk she was going to take, the sort of a needless risk the under-ground, and Jan would not approve.

She walked steadily up the hill, feeling lonely now that the quiet farmer and the old horse had vanished into the dark and the snow. I'm going to walk up, she thought, just walk up. If they stop me, I'll have to think of what to say; I won't think of it before.

The guard box was empty. She went up the drive, and by the round tower, and through an archway into the courtyard; she kept on walking until she came to a side door of the church. No one challenged her. She appeared to be entirely alone in the silent world of snow. She did not stop to think that Germans made much of Christmas as a jolly party, and were so superconfident that they'd take themselves to warmer places, with their comrades, than old cold cathedrals. She thought it was sort of a miracle. After all, it was Christmas Eve.

The cathedral was dark, and high, and cold, and silent. She wished for a candle, even just one candle to light. She knelt by a pillar and crossed her hands. For a long time, it was peaceful.

Then she prayed, "Dear God, make Pawel well again. Come with us to find help in England. Be with us on our trip. Remember our dear Poland. And everyone who lives and fights for freedom and peace."

That was rather a selfish prayer, she thought, but she was cold now, and suddenly frightened again. As she stood up, she said loudly, "King Boleslas of Poland, it is time to call your knights to help us. After all, Grandmother Zofia used to say God helps those who help themselves. Come and help your own Poland."

She felt childish, a little silly, and very reassured. As the moon penetrated the snowclouds and shot a shaft of light through the stained-glass windows above, she was almost certain she saw Boleslas the Valiant of a thousand years ago, Henry the Pious, and Ladislas the Short, and King Casimir who was called Great, and around them a great army of knights in shining armor, men of letters and of bible and of sword. She saw them and then she thought, all who sleep in the Wavel will surely fight now.

"Amen." She knelt again for a moment. And then she hurried out and away, because Dr. Jerzy and Zosia were coming back to Wit's little cottage for Christmas, and perhaps she could go with them.

17

It was a few mornings later that Jan paused on the heights of a pass in the Tatras to wait for Wanda. Far below were the valleys and foothills, the silver glint of a frozen river where it was windswept, and the green of the forest where snow had blown off the pines.

In the dusk, they would slip down the other side of the mountain—if all went well—into Czechoslovakia.

Jan felt a choking urge to turn his skis and slide down his own trail back home again, back to the lands that were familiar and dear despite the occupying enemy. Now Wanda caught up with him, breathless from the ascent, her face hot, her eyes full of tears from the cold. She turned to look back too.

The little train that had brought them from Krakow had long since vanished into the valleys of the foothills. Dr. Jerzy had traveled with them and given them the plan of their route, money, and the names of the people they should contact. His last words had been, "You are now Poland's accredited ambassadors. Whatever you do, whatever you say, remember you represent Poland."

As she remembered his quick warm hug and a kiss to both of them, Wanda thought, if I stand here another minute I'll run home again. Old Wit had made a pair of skis for each of them as a loving surprise. It had been the first big Christmas present any of them had received since the occupation. They'd have to go right now, or she'd go back home!

"How will we know when we've crossed the border, Jan?"

"There is a treeless belt across the hills. When we cross that, we'll have left Poland."

Jan pushed ahead again, breaking the trail. Over his shoulder, he said, "Jerzy says the guard is lax here. It's cold, and it's Christmastime. All the same, we'd better be careful."

It was beginning to snow. That would hide their tracks. It was cold, powdery snow, fast for skiing, good for going away; but nothing would ease the pain in her heart, Wanda knew, as she followed Jan's quick descent. He stopped after a time.

"Do you realize we are across?" He spoke through the frost on the cap that covered his chin as well as his forehead. "And see, that blue streak rising above the trees? That's smoke. It ought to be from Farmer Mietek's cabin. Just follow me. We'll be there in an hour."

Wanda was too tired to talk. She thought she'd count. Up to a hundred, then to a thousand, then to another thousand; surely, soon they would be there.

Jan was shaking her. "Wanda! Wanda! We are here!"

Her feet kept going on. Her hands felt frozen to the ski poles.

A big man emerged from the darkness. His sheepskin coat was frosted and prickly. He picked her up and carried her inside. Jan knocked the snow off the skis and carried them in too. There was a huge, flat-topped stove along the middle wall. The heat was the first thing Wanda felt. Then, there was a short, fat woman in an apron and a friendly voice.

"There, little one, brave one," the voice crooned. Someone was rubbing her hands and feet and face and she fell asleep.

When she awakened, she was in a high bed in the corner of a room. Firelight was glancing off wooden beams of the ceiling and on the blackened walls. There were shelves with gay pottery on them; it was like long ago. She turned her head, hoping the dream wouldn't go, and there was Jan on a footstool by the fire, and an old man with a beard, and a girl, knitting.

She began to hear the old man's words.

". . . they come over the hills and we try to have something for them to eat. Young Hela here knits socks and mittens from the wool of our own lambs. We hide the animals in mountain pastures and have kept them at least this long. The news is good, young friend. The Allies have landed in North Africa. The Russians are holding firm at Stalingrad. Meanwhile, here, we have shot a few bear, and the partisans coming through have been glad of strong food. I hear it's been thin living on the plains below."

"We've hardly anything left in Poland," Jan said. "The Germans have taken everything, even the seed grain, now that they are not doing so well on the Russian front. The first winter of the war when the Nazis came, most of the Poles burned everything they couldn't wear or hide. You know, rather than give it to the enemy. Since then, we've had nothing new. This at least happened in Warsaw, and I've heard it happened all over Poland."

"We have been better off here in the Tatras," the old man said. "We aid our own and bedevil the enemy. Hela here has been reading a children's paper which one of the men making his way out to join the freedom forces left behind. So when a Nazi patrol came by she followed the instructions in the paper; she acted stupid. She alerted the men in the hills. Following her wrong instructions not a single Nazi came out of the trap to denounce her. We were proud of her, and she a small girl."

"What paper was that?" Jan asked.

"Get it, girl," Farmer Mietek said. "It had queer writing on top. Music, I should guess. I play the violin myself, but I can't make any sense of written music."

Wanda climbed out of the high bed. The girl handed her a worn paper, one they had themselves written and printed, months old. Jan looked over her shoulder. They smiled at one another. Then, they sang the "Polonaise" for the old man.

"That's a fine tune," he said. "Fetch me my fiddle, dear girl, will you now?"

He tucked the violin under his chin, and following Jan's clear whistling was soon playing the entire "Polonaise" as though he was following written music.

He looked very pleased. "Now that I hear the whole of it," he said, "I do recall that quite a few men going through here in the late fall of 1939 were singing this very song."

Earnestly he played through the "Polonaise" again.

"Scraps of uniforms they were wearing," he said, "but their courage was made of whole cloth. They were on their way, they said, to join the Free Polish Forces on the outside and continue the fight."

The next morning he harnessed his horse and took Jan and Wanda to the village in the valley. There they were to get on a local train which would take them to the city of Zilina in Czechoslovakia. If anyone questioned them, Dr. Jerzy had instructed them to say they were going from their home in a border village to stay with an uncle. Farmer Mietek and Hela waited until the train pulled out.

"He's probably the last Pole we'll see for a long time." Wanda flattened her nose against the window and waved frantically.

"We'll be coming back. The war can't last forever," Jan said.

The conductor barely glanced at their tickets as he went through the carriage. They looked like the rest of the poorly clad, thin, country folk that used the rural train to cross the border.

In Zilina it was still easy to make themselves understood. Jan looked at the map Dr. Jerzy had given him, and they made their way to a street of old houses on the outskirts of the town.

"Look out for Number 45," he told Wanda. "And if there isn't a number we are to ask for Frantisek Novak."

There was a number all right, but the windows were boarded up, and the door hung on one hinge. They knocked on it, and knocked, until a woman looked out of a window next door.

"What do you kids want?" she shouted. She

was dirty, and her eyes looked everywhere but at them.

Jan took off his cap. "We are looking for Frantisek Novak."

"I don't like the look of her," Wanda whispered.

At that moment, a small boy, Kazio's size, ran up to them.

"Follow me," he said softly. "She's no good. Come on, quickly. That one will tell the Germans. The Gestapo has got Mr. Novak."

He ran on, and they ran after him. A small black and white dog joined them.

"Here," the little boy said, "come on."

He led them through a courtyard into a house and out again by the back door. On another street he slowed to a walk.

"She'll tell the Nasties, that one," he said. "I guess you'd better come home with me. I'm Jiri Uhlir, and this is my dog Yurka, and my father is a friend of Mr. Novak. That's why I was around, to warn people who might ask for him."

"Thank you very much," Jan said, "but it might be dangerous as well for you to have us. We are Poles, you see."

"That's all right," Jiri said cheerfully. "My father has Polish friends too. He doesn't know I know, but I do. My brother, Karel, has to go to a German school and he hates it, and I know that he does something dangerous himself, though he doesn't know I know. People often think little kids

146

are stupid, but we aren't. We can hear things as well as anybody."

He led the way to a small house, set back from the street, and then he ran ahead. They could hear him chattering away.

A thin, gentle-looking woman came to the doorway. Behind her, they could see a tall boy staring at them suspiciously.

"I hear you are Polish," Jiri's mother said. "Welcome, children."

147

18

Jan slept that night in Karel's room. Karel was Jiri's older brother, the only one of the family who had not made them feel welcome.

Jan's anxiety for tomorrow kept him awake. He could hear Karel tossing in his bed. Finally, he whispered, "Karel? Karel, what is it? Are you worried because we are here?"

There was a long silence in the dark room. Then the Czech boy said, "It isn't that, now. When I saw you I *was* afraid you were spies. The Nazis have many spies, and today I couldn't complete an errand I had to do. That is why I'm scared."

Suddenly Jan felt he could trust Karel. "Wanda and I," he said, "and a lot of others, many of them much younger than we are, have been working in the Polish underground, so perhaps I could help you?"

Again, there was a long silence. Then, Karel slipped across the room and crouched at the end of Jan's bed. He began to whisper.

"I haven't told my parents about this. I didn't want to worry them. But all winter I've been getting a bottle, once or twice a week, from a boy in my class. His eldest brother is a chemist, so you see he might be suspected, so I was chosen to take the bottle to a man who works in a factory. I think that the chemical in the bottle rusts joints and axles. Sabotage, you see. This afternoon he wasn't at the corner where we meet. Nor was there a message from him, as usual, when he can't come.

"Something must have happened." There was a sob in his voice. "And I'm afraid if they track me, they'll take us all. I've heard terrible stories."

"If they'd known about you they'd have come by now." Jan tried to sound confident. "Don't worry any longer. Tomorrow, we'll find someone who'll know how to use your bottle."

The next morning when they were having their breakfast of ersatz coffee and black bread, Mrs. Uhlir said, "It's dangerous for strangers in our city these days so we'll pretend that you are members of our family—should anyone ask. Remember now, you've come from my brother in the hills."

149

"I shall try to arrange something for you during the day," worried Mr. Uhlir said with a sigh.

After the boys went off on their own, Mother Uhlir wrapped a loaf of bread in an old towel and said to Wanda, "Let's go and see if we can find anything in the shops for supper."

But first, they stopped at a small house down the street and left the bread. "It's for old Mrs. Metzel," she explained. "They are Jews and they can't buy in most of the stores, nor have they been able to get work since the occupation. The neighbors give what they can."

They stopped at another house, and Mother Uhlir gave some money to the woman who came to the door. "It's difficult to save much," she said apologetically as they went on. "My husband earns less now and everything is so much more expensive. I don't tell him about this—not to worry him—so don't you mention it. That woman has three small children. Her eldest son is with the Czech Army in England, and her husband was taken to a concentration camp six months ago. We didn't have a chance to fight, you know, when the Germans marched in, as you did in Poland, but each year the occupation is getting harsher, life harder."

Early shopping hours in the city were reserved for the Germans. That meant that by the time the Czechs were allowed to go to the market, there was very little left to buy. However, today they were lucky enough to get some potatoes and two pounds of turnips.

150

Mother Uhlir pointed out to Wanda how the Czech street names had been painted out and German words splashed across. "But of course among ourselves we still call our streets by their right names," she said.

They'd walked to the far end of the town searching for food, so they took a tram home. It was crowded. Suddenly a man at the back of the tram started to sing a Czech song. Immediately, all the chattering ceased. He sang loudly and well. Four Germans in uniform, in the front of the tram, were somehow so tightly hemmed in by the rest of the passengers they couldn't get at the singing man.

He finished the song and jumped off. The tram put on speed. The Germans were swearing and shouting. The passengers looked suddenly as though there was sunlight inside them though none of them spoke or even smiled.

"That was very dangerous for everyone, not only for him," Mother Uhlir said to Wanda as they got off. "But it is the sort of danger that's worth the risk. It keeps up our spirits, our hope."

When they got home they were met by a white-faced Jiri.

"What is it, Jirushka?" Mother Uhlir hugged the little boy.

"The Nazis want Yurka." Jiri tried to keep his voice steady, though he had to swallow hard. "There are notices all over saying all dogs must be turned in."

"We'll try to hide him. Where is he now?"

"I put him into a cupboard," Jiri said, "with my coat."

They were laughing at his solution when Jan and Karel arrived. They too looked anxious.

"I think we better stay home today," Karel said. "There was some sabotage on the railways last night and the Nazis are on a rampage. They've patrols out rounding up boys to send to their slave training camps. We were stopped but I said we were taking a message to the Hussar's Mess. A boy in my class told me that trick. But it might not work a second time."

"They say they are sending hundreds of Czech boys and girls to these camps to teach them to become useful German workers," Jan told Wanda.

"To become slaves," Karel said furiously. "We know of these camps. There are Dutch boys and Norwegians, Ukrainians, Lithuanians, Estonians and Latvians, French, and Poles there. The Jews they kill, but the rest of us are supposed to become a class of slaves to serve Germans."

Mrs. Uhlir sighed. "Yes. Stay at home today. We will talk to your father when he comes home."

All day, Karel worried about his uncompleted errand, Jan about how he and Wanda were to continue their urgent trip, Jiri about his small dog, Yurka, and Mother Uhlir about worrying her husband.

But when Father Uhlir came home in the

evening, he was walking straight and looking proud. He gave his wife a hug, and he put his hand on Karel's shoulder.

"I contacted the underground today," he said. "I have tried to have nothing to do with them because I thought your safety ought to be my chief concern. I went to them only because our young Polish friends need their help. And what do I learn!

"I find out that my family are better patriots than I am. When I gave my name they greeted me warmly, not for my sake but for yours. Karel, with his ready willingness to help, is on the list of patriots. All will honor him when our land is free again. And you, Mother, are on the honor list. They say you help everyone you can."

They sat down to their simple dinner and it seemed sumptuous. Their happiness was bright. They were all working for the same cause; surely, they would win in the end.

"Jan and Wanda will be going tonight," Father Uhlir explained after they had eaten. "You have not come the direct route, I suppose, because this has been the only secure escape tunnel up until now. But the contacts are broken. However, a man from the underground has permission to use his truck, so he will take you where it will be possible for you to board a train, perhaps directly to Budapest."

"I hoped they would stay longer," little Jiri said.

"The next time." Wanda managed a smile.

They were never to forget that night. The quiet goodbyes to the kindly, courageous Uhlirs. The strangers who spoke a language they no longer understood. The long ride in the old truck down dark and bumpy roads, the many sudden stops. The fear.

There was a tinge of red in the eastern sky when they were being hurried through a maze of a freight yard. Then, by barely seen gestures and hissed commands, they were thrust into a small space under a load of bricks. At the last moment before their hiding place was closed with more bricks, a hand reached in and pushed at them a bottle, a sausage, and half a loaf of bread.

They heard shouting and commands, whistles and groaning of wheels, and then they felt a jerky movement which threw them together.

Wanda whispered, "There's a rug here. We'll share it."

"There's a little air coming through the bricks. We had better not speak."

The journey went on forever. At one stage, they opened the bottle and found it contained watered coffee. With his pocket knife, Jan cut slices of sausage and bread, but the sausage was so salty he whispered to Wanda not to eat much. It might make them too thirsty.

It was probably the next evening when a small man, black with coal dust, scratched at the bricks. The anxiety in his voice was more understandable than his words. They followed him without a question. What else could they do?

This time their hiding place was another freight car, in a box hidden underneath a load of coal. There was a blanket roll there and a couple of old car seats. Before the anxious small man covered up the way they had gone in, he handed them a large jug of water. Someone, speaking Polish, whispered to them about a hole in the corner of their box, but added not to use it except when the train was moving. They were obviously not the first passengers in this secret cubbyhole of darkness.

In the end they must have slept because it was still, or again, dark and very cold when Jan felt someone shaking him.

"Wake up," the voice urged. "You must hurry. You leave here. The cars are being uncoupled."

Jan tried to stretch himself but there wasn't enough room. He put up his hand and felt the boards that had held up the ton of coal above them. Wanda had had a nightmare that it was falling. He shook her.

Her breath came in gasps, and when his hand touched her face, it was sweaty and hot.

The voice outside was anxious. "You must come now. Soon it will be dawn. We must get you away immediately."

"Wanda, Wanda." She woke up as he began to pull her out. She stumbled and the man outside caught her. It was another railway yard, and he hurried them through the many slanting shadows.

"Our contact here is broken," he whispered. "Many of our men have been captured and shot. We had a request up the line to look after you, but there's no one to do it. I must go back with the train today or the last link will be broken."

"Where are we?" Jan asked.

"Why, in Budapest. Hungary. That's where you were going."

Slowly Jan's brain began to work. He remembered that inside the lining of his jacket were sewn a bundle of Hungarian *pengos* and an address. Jerzy had two aunts in the city.

"We'll manage," he said, "if you could only get us to an address in Buda. We may get help there."

"Wait here. I must find a friend to see to your first-class compartment. Someone else may need it."

Wanda had slipped to the ground. Even half asleep and ill, she was trying to stifle her cough. Jan ripped the top of the pocket in his lining and pulled out the slip of paper Jerzy had given him.

He had it ready when their coal-dust camouflaged friend came back. He lit a match inside his cap and read it. He was silent a long time.

"Sure this is the right place?" he said slowly. "You know the Hungarians are cooperating with the Germans? This is a swanky address. Houses are called palaces there, and a lot of people there are collaborators."

"The address was given to us by a patriot," Jan said. "And look at Wanda. She's not well. I must get her somewhere to rest, eat."

The man made up his mind.

"You've got sound references," he said. "Come on."

Walking quickly, both of them supporting Wanda, they went the tricky ways Jan and Wanda could never have found alone. Then there were lights in the city and lights on the bridges, something Jan hadn't seen at night for years. Like a black velvet path, a river reflected them.

"Look, boy, that is the Danube," the unknown man said. "We are in Pest, those are the hills of Buda. That makes Budapest. I cannot go with you further."

"Thank you," Jan said. He put out his hand and the man gave it a firm grip. "We'll meet again in peace."

19

Jan awoke in a huge canopied bed, a silk eiderdown over him. He couldn't remember where he was or how he had got there. He lay staring at the oak paneled room, at the streak of sunlight coming through thick, faded, velvet curtains.

One, two, three, four, he said to himself. Start at the beginning. The kind Czechs, the train, the dirt, the discomfort, Wanda being ill. Wanda! He sat up. That's what had happened.

The terrible walk, trying to hold up Wanda, knowing that if they were stopped he wouldn't know a word of Hungarian, wondering if the address he had was the right one, fearing that the old aunts had died. Finally there had been the tall house with the address that was the same as on Jerzy's note, but with no lights, and the shutters closed. If Wanda hadn't collapsed on the steps, he would not have gone up them.

He'd rung the bell. It seemed a long time before an old man, a liveried jacket on top of his night shirt, had opened the door.

Jan, conscious of his shabby clothes, his dirty face and uncombed hair, stood very straight.

"Will you please help Miss Wanda," he said in Polish. "She is not well. I come from the nephew of the Countess Magahazy."

The old man took his time, staring at them. Finally he called over his shoulder. A sleepy looking old woman appeared from the end of the hall and helped Wanda in.

The old man said, "I am Tibor. This way, young sir."

The old man had spoken in Polish but with a foreign accent. Jan didn't remember undressing or washing, but he couldn't see his clothes anywhere and his hands were clean. He jumped up, pulled the curtains, and looked at himself in the mirror. His face was clean too.

There was a water jug and a basin in the corner of the room, and Jan washed himself vigorously all over. The soap was scented. He hadn't seen anything like it for years. But where were his clothes! There was a silk dressing gown, and though he hated to wear someone else's clothes, he put it on. He'd have to find Wanda.

There was a knock on the door.

"In!" Jan shouted angrily. He had failed. He had fallen asleep before he knew where he was. Before he had seen Wanda was all right. Before he was certain they had arrived at a safe place. He was furious with himself.

Old Tibor, now immaculate in worn but clean livery, came in.

"The Madame and her sister are at breakfast," he said. "They would like you to join them."

"Where is Wanda?" Jan demanded. "Where are my clothes?"

"The young lady is in bed. My daughter is with her at the moment and the doctor has been here. She has a high temperature. She keeps calling for someone named Pawel." Tibor looked curiously at Jan. "We are trying to, ah, clean your clothes."

"I can't go like this!" Jan said. "And I had a letter. . . ."

Tibor nodded toward the dressing table. There was the bundle of *pengos* and Dr. Jerzy's letter to his aunts.

"I regret to say the young sir's clothes came, ah, somewhat apart when they were being cleaned." Tibor stared steadily ahead. "There is a wardrobe of the ladies' great-great nephew, which, if you would be good enough to choose from, is, ah, here."

160

"My own clothes are good enough for me."
Polish pride is touchy and Jan's was one of the
touchiest.

"The ladies are expecting you." For the first
time, the old man looked directly at Jan. "They are
very, very old."

"All right," Jan said. "If they will receive me
like this."

"The ladies do not come down any longer."
Tibor led the way up a grand staircase. "They have
not left their suite for some years."

While Jan was puzzling over this remark,
Tibor opened a door and motioned him to enter.
Wintry sunlight flooded an old-fashioned over-
crowded room. It looked somewhat like an antique
shop. Two very ancient ladies sat at a table by a
bow window. They were fragile old ladies with pink
and white faces, powdered hair, ruffles fell down
their faded pink and pale blue peignoirs and fluttered about their wrists.

Jan bowed. "I am Jan Kolenko," he said. "I
come with greetings from Poland and from Dr.
Jerzy of Krakow. Thank you for taking us in."

The two old ladies looked at him and twittered at one another.

Then the one in pale blue said, "Come,
come, young man. Your breakfast is getting cold."

Tibor served them silently and capably.
Through the window, Jan could see beautiful,
faded houses sloping down the hill to the River

161

Danube, and beyond the river, the low shore of Pest. The moment was dreamlike.

The little old ladies lived in a world of their own, Jan realized. Every time he tried to explain his predicament, one or the other began to chatter in gay, birdlike voices of matters long ago. Sofia, the countess, had married a Magahazy; Fina hadn't married at all. There had been years when they used to return to spend summers in the Polish mountains; sometimes, the years didn't seem that long ago at all; sometimes, they faded. How old would Jerzy, dear boy, be now? He was always too thin. He was their grandnephew. Tibor would know! Tibor would come to Poland too; he had even married a girl from their family estate. And, of course, Jan and the little girl—she had a cold, had she not—could stay as long as they wished. Jan felt the dream turning into a nightmare. There would be no help for them here.

After an endless time, they dismissed him very sweetly. They hoped he would be happy staying with them. Tibor would look after him.

In the passage, Jan turned to the old man. "What is happening here?" he demanded.

"The ladies have forgotten there is a war on in the world," the old man said. "Their interest is in the past."

"But what about us?" Jan began, and stopped. Quite possibly, they had walked into a trap. If only Wanda hadn't been so ill.

162

Tibor looked at Jan piercingly. "The ladies are Polish by birth."

He seemed about to say more, but he turned instead and led Jan up another staircase. "The young lady is here. The doctor said she should rest."

It was a pleasant room but it smelled as though it hadn't been used for a long time. Wanda was in a vast four poster bed. Her face was flushed.

"I'm awfully sorry," she said hoarsely. "I feel awful. I shouldn't have come. The doctor says I should stay in bed a week, more."

"Try, *try* to get well," Jan said. "Dr. Jerzy's aunts, poor old things, are completely gaga. They won't be of any help; they think it's a hundred years ago. And I don't know if we can trust Tibor."

"I am sorry, Jan, so sorry." Wanda's eyes filled with tears.

"Never mind," Jan said. "I'll accept the clothes they are offering to lend me and I'll go into town and see if I can make a contact. There must be someone somewhere. This was only an address in an emergency. But don't you worry. Just try to get well."

"Pawel," Wanda sobbed.

"Never mind," Jan said again. "I'll find a way."

During the days that followed, from early morning to late night, Jan walked the lovely streets of Budapest. If only, he thought, he could understand the language. He scanned all the faces he

163

passed, he tried to listen hard, but everywhere there were Germans in their uniforms, and the Hungarians speaking their quite incomprehensible language. He felt he couldn't take the risk of speaking to a stranger not only because of Wanda, but also because of the vague old ladies who had given them shelter.

After one evening of his fruitless search, he'd let himself into the house and was climbing the staircase to his room when he heard the whistled tones of the "Polonaise." Wanda! Perhaps in danger.

He rushed about opening doors along a long corridor.

The third one opened on to a big dusty room. Wanda was wrapped in blankets, sunk in a huge chair. There was a grand piano under the bow windows that fronted the house on all stories.

"I whistled," Wanda smiled, "because I recognized your footsteps on the stairs."

"Are you feeling any better?"

"I will be, if you'll play the 'Polonaise'."

He didn't want to. His heart was full of disappointment, fear, and annoyance at her for getting ill so inconveniently. Then he remembered all they had gone through together, and little Pawel, and the rest of their friends. He had decided, on the way back from his unsuccessful walk, that he would go on alone, and he knew he'd have to tell her that. But first he'd play for her.

He went to the piano. It was in tune, surprisingly. With a sigh he adjusted the piano stool and turned and smiled at her. Then the familiar loved chords of the "Polonaise" filled the room.

Tibor was standing inside the door when he finished.

"You should have played the music when you came," the old man said ruefully. "We were told that would be the sign. I even opened the music room on purpose. We had to be sure, naturally."

Jan stared at the old man, open-mouthed.

"You are wondering what I have to do with this, young sir. You have seen the ladies. Years and sorrow have taken their toll. For some time I have handled the business they started. Transportation to Yugoslavia has been arranged for you but you do realize, *we had to be sure.*"

The next morning they went to say goodbye to the old ladies.

Wanda forgot her manners to stare with curiosity at precisely the scene of a breakfast table by a high window that Jan had described; hadn't they moved at all? Countess Magahazy lifted her lorgnette and gave her stare for stare.

"Amazing," she said. "Don't you find it so, Fina?"

The other old lady twittered eagerly, "She is, of course, shorter, and younger, and a girl, but you are quite right, Sofia. Amazing."

"I thought so too," said old Tibor unexpectedly.

"You remind us of someone," the Countess told Wanda kindly. "A charming young man, a cavalry officer. He stopped here for a time, didn't he, Tibor?"

"In the late autumn of 1939, Madame. On his way from Poland to England. He helped to organize the railway, if you remember, Madame."

"Quite right, Tibor. Yes, though of course it wasn't a railway at all. So many of them came and went. Captain Denin, that was his name."

"But I am Wanda Denin," Wanda said slowly. "My father?"

"Yes, little miss." Tibor spoke softly behind them. "He spoke of the little daughter he had had to leave behind. We couldn't have managed the organization without his help. He knew many people here and despite the risk, he remained for several months and got the underground railway and alternatives going. He longed to return to Poland but his orders were to see to an escape route and then join his general in London."

The old ladies twittered to one another as Tibor showed Jan and Wanda out of the room.

"They have been very brave," he said gravely, "but too much has happened to them. They prefer to forget. Yet I am certain they know what a good cover they make for the help we have been able to give from this house to all who continue to fight for freedom. And here is my granddaughter, Poldi. She will take you on your way."

166

Jan put out his hand. "How can we thank you, Tibor?"

"No thanks are needed," the old man said. "Go with God's speed. Come back if the Fates will it."

20

Captain Milan spoke sharply to the frontier guard. He was a tiny man with a dark, sad face and arrogant voice. He had on the German approved "Ustasa" Yugoslavian uniform, worn by collaborationists. Jan, dressed in a Hungarian river patrol uniform, watched the Yugoslav border guards wave their boat on and out of Hungary.

Their voyage down the Danube, "Duna" as the Hungarians called the legendary river, had been as implausible as everything that had happened since they'd left dear, familiar Poland.

Tibor's granddaughter had brought them to this smart icebreaker patrol boat, moored, curiously enough, at a Yacht Club outside Budapest instead of at a military wharf. They'd found fur-lined coats and boots already on board for them, and the short, arrogant Captain Milan. He was the only one on board who spoke Polish, and he hadn't told them much.

Now, he smiled for the first time. "Well, we appeared to have foxed the Nazis again. We'll have to get off soon. The boat must return to Budapest before it is missed, and you two and I must get lost."

"We got the lift because of you, sir?" Jan asked.

"We give lifts to worthy passengers when we can. One never expected the hundreds of little yacht clubs along the Danube to turn out to be so useful. You came at an opportune moment and with good references. Can I be of further service to you?"

Jan and Wanda had been as uncommunica-tive as the little captain. Now Jan felt the time had come to speak.

"We are on our way to England. We thought of trying to make for the Adriatic coast be-cause—because we have heard of possibilities of going on from there."

Captain Milan laughed shortly. "I have no-ticed you are not blabbermouths. Good. You had better come with me. I must report in at the capi-tal. A bold manner is safer than a false mustache. Get ready. We have a cold drive ahead."

There was a car waiting for them when they docked briefly by a small quay. The patrol boat was away, turning to go back up the river before they were in the car.

It was only a short drive to a deserted-looking wooden station. A train chugged up before they had waited ten minutes. Obviously, Captain Milan believed in instant timing. His haughty officiousness so flustered the conductor he didn't even ask for Jan's or Wanda's papers. The uniformed Germans on the train paid them no attention either. The captain's collaborationist uniform was as good as a passport.

As they neared Belgrade, the captain spoke softly, without any arrogance at all. "We'll soon be in Beli Grad—the White Town—today called Beograd. Seventeen times in 300 years my city has been destroyed. Sixteen times we have rebuilt it. When peace comes we will rebuild it for the seventeenth time. Here the River Sava joins the Danube. There is the lovely bastion of Kalamegdan under which the two mighty waters meet; it was built by the enemy during the Turkish occupation. You have never seen such a city!"

Wanda nudged Jan. "Remember Dr. Jerzy! According to him, there was never such a city as Krakow!"

Jan grinned. "According to you, *Warsaw* is the loveliest."

Captain Milan went on. "Here in Belgrade the east and the west meet. We have great, new, modern buildings now, but ah, I do love the old taverns by the Terazye Square, with the lanterns swinging by the sunken doorways and the sound of the *gusle*."

Suddenly, he was on his feet. He peered out the window, alert, wary. The platform was lined with German soldiers, their eyes scanning the windows of the slowing train.

"Remember. *Terazye Square. The Albanian café. Tonight.* Get out fast. Mingle in the crowd. Make for the center of the city. Take care. Tonight."

He was running down the carriage. At the far end, he threw another glance out of the window. Then he was through the doorway.

"I hope he makes it," Jan muttered, but his heart had sunk into his boots. They were on their own again. He reached for their one small bag. He felt Wanda's hand in his.

Then they were in the rush of passengers pushing out of the carriage. The Germans were obviously not looking for them; their frowning faces ignored the crowd of peasants around them. Even the ticket takers only waved them on, out of the way. Jan pulled Wanda briskly out to the strange streets, strange city, Belgrade.

Captain Milan had said the language would not be difficult for them and he was right. If they listened carefully, they could understand much of it, and if they spoke slowly, the Yugoslavians understood them.

But it had been a long, lonesome day by the time they found Terazye Square. Though a lot of the rubble of 1941 bombings had been cleared away, it was still partly in ruins. In an odd way the signs of German destruction here in a foreign city made Jan and Wanda feel suddenly more at home. Here as in Warsaw, brave people had fought for their freedom and were continuing the fight. All they had to do to be among friends was to find a way into the underground.

Captain Milan was their way.

They found the Albanian tavern with a lantern swinging by the door and a few steps leading below the street level. They sat down at a table by the doorway to wait. Jan ordered a spiced stew which obviously had more vegetables and maize than meat, but it warmed them. Thoughtful, thorough Jerzy had given him a few *dinars* with which he could pay for it.

Their eyes grew tired of watching the door. They heard talk of curfew as the café began to empty around them. Soon, it would be dangerous to be found on the streets. Soon, the café would close.

For the hundredth time Jan's eyes strayed to the German poster on the wall of the café:

STOP AND READ! MARTIAL LAW!
ASSEMBLIES ARE PROHIBITED!
LEAVING YOUR WORK IS PROHIBITED!
GATHERING IN GROUPS ON THE STREETS
IS PROHIBITED!

But still no Captain Milan appeared.

"You are strangers?" The young girl who had served them, now dressed in a thick coat, was standing beside them. She had been watching them curiously for a long time.

Jan stood up. "Yes." He took a chance. "Polish."

"You have been waiting for someone, I think," the girl said. "They won't come now. Soon, it'll be curfew."

"We have nowhere else to go," Wanda said.

"Do you know where I am going?" The girl was bubbling over with excitement. Her black eyes were bright. "Into the hills. To join the guerrillas. Tonight!"

Why, she's younger than Wanda, Jan thought. But she seems like one of us, and she's our one chance. "Can we come with you?" he said. "We *must* get in touch with the guerrillas."

The girl clapped her hands to her mouth. It was such an instinctive gesture that they had to smile. It was as though she had said aloud "*again* I've talked too much."

Slowly she smiled back at them. "I'm Trinka," she said. "I *think* you can come, but we must check with Marko. He's my brother."

"Trinka!" A stocky dark boy came running from the back of the café. "Hurry!"

173

"Wait, Marko. We have company."

Jan stepped in front of the boy. "I'm Jan and this is Wanda," he said fiercely. "We are from Poland. We *must* find the guerrillas. *Please.*"

Marko glared at Trinka. "We haven't time to argue, and I expect I can't stop you from following us. But believe me, if you turn out to be spies, we'll kill you. That Trinka! I should have known! Come on."

They ran through the dark streets, and it was like Warsaw again. Only this time, it was Marko who hissed the warnings to be quiet, and Jan wondered if he too had sounded as abrupt and angry the times he had been worried and fearful.

Marko's haste was explained by a car waiting for them on the outskirts of Belgrade. There were a half dozen men clinging to it before it sputtered to a start. They had stolen it from the Germans, Marko explained, and Jan told him that forest guerrillas in Poland did the very same thing. Then he was silent, and Wanda knew he was remembering the escape with Stas and Kazio from the prison in Warsaw.

The dawn was white in the winter sky when Marko awakened Trinka and Wanda, who'd fallen asleep despite the bumpy drive.

"We get out here," he said shortly.

A path wound almost vertically up from the road. They heard the car start again as they began to climb. Marko had a sack over his shoulder and a strange-looking instrument under his arm.

174

"Where are we going?" Jan asked.

"The headquarters. Isn't that where you wanted to go?"

Wilderness closed in on them. High black crags, forbidding black woods, the narrow perpendicular path. The path went on and on.

At midmorning Marko stopped at a hut they hadn't even seen until they were right upon it. It looked as old as the trees and the rocks shielding it. Deftly he started a tiny fire in an open hearth. From a shelf, he took down a kettle and a pan. From his sack, he produced a few small bags.

"Trinka," he said, "we'll have some maize and herb coffee."

He wasn't even trying to be friendly, but, Jan thought, he had a right to be suspicious of them. How could he know they were friends?

Waiting for the kettle to boil, Marko picked up his odd instrument. It had only a single string, but somehow he could make a song with that. And then he saw the sudden interest in Jan's face.

"Can you play the *gusle?*" he asked.

"No," Jan said. "I've never seen one before, but I'd like to try it. Once, I played the violin a little."

"The *gusle* is the same principle." Unexpectedly Marko's voice was eager. "Look, you scoop out a block of wood, stretch a lamb skin over it. Then you put this little bridge here, and stretch a horsehair right across. See, the bow is made only of horsehair too. I made this one myself."

175

Trinka moved away from the fire leaving Wanda to look after things.

"All the old legends of Serbia have come down to us because *guslari* have sung the stories of heroic deeds. All our songs of freedom and of the mountains and happiness and sadness are always to the tune of the *gusle*. Try it, Jan."

Reluctantly Marko handed over the instrument. Jan tried and tried. He looked at Wanda and saw her tired face and thought, we'll sing them the "Polonaise." And after a time, he suddenly got the knack of it. The tune was there. As he hummed, Wanda began to sing.

"What's that?" Marko asked.

"The song of the children in the Polish underground and of all of Poland, for a long time, for that matter."

"Tell us, do tell us." Trinka had caught on to the tune.

As they ate the breakfast Wanda had got ready, they took turns telling Marko and Trinka about Poland, about Marja and Stas, Kazio, Pawel, the twins, all of them, and of their own newspaper and the experiences they had had. It seemed here, in the mountain hut, a very long time ago.

Marko got up and put his hand out to Jan. "I am sorry I did not greet you with kindness. I didn't know who you were, and Trinka is always picking up new friends. I am glad you are with us. And I am glad we are going where we are going. In an hour and a half, two hours, we'll be there!"

21

"There!" Marko paused and pointed straight ahead.

They saw nothing but trees and rocks. Then, as in a picture puzzle, their eyes began to find out-lines of buildings and stone walls, camouflaged with branches of evergreens.

"It used to be an old monastery," Marko ex-plained. "A hundred years ago or more the Turks destroyed it. Only a small part was rebuilt. After Belgrade was bombed there were so many or-phaned children they had to be cared for some-where. Someone remembered this place. The free-dom fighters took time off from attacking the

Germans to build new shelters into the ancient walls. There are nearly two hundred children here, the monks of the old monastery are the directors, and—well, you'll see."

"But Marko! I want to go with the guerrillas!" Trinka cried.

"We'll stop here," Marko said. "I've messages to give. Then we'll go deeper into the mountains. You'll get to the headquarters. Wait."

There were not only children they found, but refugees and wounded guerrillas, not only here but in many mountain monasteries such as this one. But the most interesting thing to Wanda was that the British did drop much-needed supplies such as medicines and vitamins; surely, that meant they could get some for their own Pawel too. They were anxious to be on their way.

"Today we go," Trinka shouted the third morning.

Now they headed directly south, further into the vastness of the mountains that guarded the sea. They had been lent skis and made good time. They slept at a mountain croft the first night, and though they were given lamb stew for supper, the farmer and his wife wore rags on their feet. The Germans had managed to get most of the leather, so the peasants gave their boots to the guerrillas, Marko told them. After all, it was the most valuable present they could give. They spent the next night in the log hut of an old woman whose five shepherd sons were with the freedom fighters.

Midday on the third day, a man suddenly stepped from behind a tree, blocking the children's path. Then he recognized Marko.

"*Dobar dan!*" he shouted. "Who are these with you, young friend?"

"Good day to you, Stoyan. These are friends from Poland and my horrible little sister, Trinka, who has come to join us."

"Ah, we know of the Polish travelers. Welcome, young friends." The Serbian guerrilla saluted them, waved them on, and vanished again into the trees.

"I wonder what he meant about knowing you," Marko said.

"I can't understand it, either," Jan admitted.

An hour and a half later, they skied into the encampment of Marko's company of guerrillas. It was a real hideout, half in caves, half in low barracks buildings hidden in thickets and camouflaged with bushes, branches, and snow. In a valley between the cliffs was the hospital and a camp for women and children. This is where Marko took Wanda and Trinka.

"There are so many homeless and orphaned children that even in our camps we must shelter them," Marko explained, leading Jan to his own barracks. Here Jan found some thirty boys between fourteen and sixteen years of age, training as junior guerrillas.

"We are taught Indian tricks," a small boy

called Danilo told Jan eagerly. "Like sneaking so close to the enemy you could scalp him before he saw you, hiding in the underbrush so no one can tell you from a rock, going through the forest without leaving a track. Things like that."

"We do less exciting things too," Marko laughed. "In the summer, we pick berries and mushrooms, and collect wild honey from hollow trees, and we fish and trap so that the women can preserve all these things for winter. It's our job to get the firewood and clean the barracks. Do come and see what we have right here in camp."

Marko rushed Jan on an inspection tour of workshops where tailors were patching up guerrilla uniforms, shoes were being made by people who never made shoes before, women were weaving cloth for sheets, blankets, shirts, and bandages, and blacksmiths were repairing weapons.

"We have a whole town here," Marko said proudly, "camouflaged to look like a mountainside."

"What about a newspaper?" Jan asked.

"Oh, we have that too, further up the peaks in an old shrine. There's also a powerful radio transmitter there with which we can send messages —even all the way to America."

"But no children's paper?"

Marko's eyes sparkled. "You could show us how to start one. We certainly have enough children in all the camp to read it."

180

A boy came running up the hill, shouting, "The captain wants to see the Polish boy."

Marko gave Jan a surprised stare.

"That's funny," he said. "I didn't think I could even arrange for you to meet him. He's the chief of this camp. We, the younger ones, seldom see him. He organizes the raiders and plans the attacks. But he's great. I remember soon after I first came he made a speech asking us to do our humbler tasks thoroughly and well because too soon we also would be fighting. He said, 'We have no tanks and no cannon, but our mountains are on our side. Every pass is a trap and every cliff a barricade against the Nazis. And everybody's skills are welcome, and needed.' You are honored, Jan, to be able to meet him."

They crossed from the hidden encampment of workshops, passed the barracks for the wounded hidden in the thickets, and arrived at a building, half cave, half bungalow, sheltered beneath ancient spreading spruce trees.

A big man with a leather-brown face and piercing eyes came out. Marko snapped to attention, so Jan did.

The guerrilla leader stared hard at the Polish boy.

Then he snapped at Marko, "Report!"

Briefly, accurately, Marko related how they had met. "And if he is a spy, my captain, I will kill him myself. But I don't think he is."

The captain nodded and held out his hand

to Jan. "We had a message you might be turning up."

"Could you be confusing Wanda and me with someone else?" Jan wasn't going to be accepted under false pretences. "No one knew we were coming here."

"You know Captain Milan?"

Jan's frown turned into a smile. "Oh, then he got away!"

A reluctant smile broke over the big man's stern face. "*He* always gets away," he said.

"Did he say anything, did he send a message, about our being on our way further, much further, sir?"

"Yes. I am to tell you it is being organized."

"How soon do we leave, please?"

"It depends entirely on the moon, the weather, the opportunity." He turned to Marko. "Arrange accommodation for our guests. You, Jan Kolenko, come with me. I would like news of our brothers in Poland."

For nearly three weeks, Jan and Wanda stayed in the guerrilla camp in the mountains. They were busy weeks, for no one was permitted to waste the short daylight hours. Jan joined in the daily military drilling of the older boys. Wanda helped the women with the wounded and in looking after the smallest children. She learned new ways of cooking, how camomile and other medical herbs, picked in the summer and autumn, could be used for healing, how to fold bandages, and how

182

not to cry for Pawel except at night, alone in her bunk. She also drilled with the older girls who would be going on patrol with the guerrilla troops when they were needed.

Marko got permission from his group leader to get a children's newspaper started. He picked half a dozen eager volunteers (he was more interested in fighting), and Jan and Wanda told them the problems there would be about printing a children's paper. They had been loaned the use of a printing press in the camp at Black Peak, higher up the mountain, and had printed the first issue the day the message arrived that they were to get ready immediately to travel down the mountains to the coast.

When the time came to say goodbye, it seemed that most of the people in camp turned out to see them off. There was a lot of handshaking and backslapping. Only Trinka was nowhere in sight.

Their guide, the sturdy young guerrilla called Stoyan, kept hurrying them. "A long way to go. Must leave now. Now!"

"We *can't* leave without saying goodbye to Trinka." Wanda stood her ground. "After all, who knows what might have happened to us, except for her!"

"True enough," Jan agreed. "I'll try something. Marko, please, lend me your *gusle* just for a moment."

Marko ran to fetch it. Jan whispered to Wanda.

Then he sat down, cross-legged, on the snow
like a true *guslari* and touched out the melancholy,
monotonous wail of the one-stringed fiddle. He
nodded to Wanda.

Together they sang, as he played the accom-
paniment, the old Serbian song Trinka had taught
them:

> "The night is my protector,
> My cover the moonlit sky;
> Stones make up my bedstead
> And the pillows where I lie. . . ."

And there was Trinka suddenly, in tears, of
course, but hugging them and wishing them luck.

As they started down the mountain track,
they got a surprise that nearly made them cry too.
Everyone started to sing the "Polonaise"!

Jan had played it and was allowed to whistle
it at work, and many of the musical Serbs had easily
learned the melody. Now it echoed and reechoed
around Jan and Wanda in these Yugoslav hills—
the song they had brought with them from Poland
as their dearest possession.

Wanda rubbed her eyes and whispered, "I'll
miss them all."

"We'll come back when the war is won,"
Jan said huskily.

Where the track came down to a road, a car
waited for them.

"Captain Milan sent it," Stoyan explained.
"I've never known anyone to be able to pick up

cars the way he does. I doubt the Germans have any left."

As they were getting into the car, there was a crash in the woods behind them and Marko slid down the path, red-faced and breathless.

"I want you to have this," he said, pushing his *gusle* into Jan's hand. Then he was scrambling up the path again and was lost in the trees.

Stoyan looked at the instrument in Jan's hand.

"A Serb never gives his *gusle* away," he said slowly and started the car. "Except to a friend."

They saw the sea from the heights in the twilight. The blue Adriatic was gray this wintry evening. Behind them were the peaks and below were the slopes of the great hills. In the summer, they would be magnificently beautiful; now they loomed frightening, forbidding.

They drove down the hairpin turns with reckless speed. It was dark when the car finally turned in at high gates. They couldn't see the house in the pitch-blackness as the driver flicked off the car lights. Then a door was flung open and a rectangular area of faint light framed the silhouette of a dapper little man.

"So you didn't do so badly on your own!" Captain Milan's voice rang out. "Sorry to have left you so abruptly and not to have kept our appointment. I was rather on the hop that night. Come in, come in."

There was a meal set on the table, richer

than any they had seen for a long time. There was spaghetti and cold meat, bread, and honey, and goat's milk. As they ate, Captain Milan sat down with them, talking, questioning, not arrogant at all, but like an old friend.

They had finished when three tall, fair men came into the room.

"These are Englishmen." Captain Milan introduced them. "They have been visiting our guerrilla camps as liaison officers. A ship is coming to pick them up tonight. I thought that would be a good chance for you."

One of the strangers grinned at Jan and Wanda and said in halting Polish, "So you are the two we have been hearing about. Quite a trip you've had. We'll be glad to give you a lift the rest of the way."

"You are going by boat to the coast of Italy," Captain Milan explained, "then by military route to England; that is, you will embark for Africa, from there you'll fly to Lisbon in Portugal, and on to London. But now come with me. You can rest until four. Then we will see if we can get you away." He smiled, and suddenly they liked him tremendously.

Wanda was still drowsy with sleep when they started on their last Yugoslavian adventure. The house, they discovered, was on a cliff above the Adriatic. A path from the terrace led down to a cove.

The night was still pitch black, but they

186

could hear the susurrant sea as they stood waiting on the shore. Captain Milan lit a cigarette inside his hat. He must have kept it there for they couldn't see it glow.

After a long while, a green light winked twice in the darkness.

Captain Milan waved his cigarette in an arch.

"Time to get into the boats." He helped Wanda in. The oarlocks must have been wrapped in rags for there was no sound as the captain began to row. No one spoke. Then the green light winked almost on top of them.

"Are you there, you blokes?" a voice asked in a language Jan and Wanda recognized as English from nearly forgotten lessons at school.

"Right here," a man from the second boat answered. "Give a hand, fellows. There are two children coming up first."

"Over here. Get a move on, this is an unhealthy spot tonight. The Heinies are buzzing about like wasps."

Strong hands were pulling Wanda up. Jan felt his arm taken. Then he was going up a rope ladder and the ship swayed against him.

Below, in the darkness, Captain Milan's voice came clearly and warmly across the sounds of the sea, "God be with you! Safe voyage, friends."

22

There would still be snow around Old Wit's cottage and under the trees in the park to the castle, Wanda thought. If the cottage was still there, and if the castle was still there, and if everyone was still there.

Through the window at which she stood, Wanda could see a park where daffodils came through the green grass and trees were burgeoning. Though it was only March, in the ruins of this strange city of London, flowers were already in bloom. It would be a long time yet before spring came to Poland and brought out the flowers in the ruins of Warsaw.

It had taken them a long time to make the trip, and what good was it, after all? She glanced at a clock like one her English aunts had had, on top of the mantelpiece. Here too, the fireplace could not be lit, because there were shortages of coal, and strict blackouts. Surely, Jan would be home soon.

The waste of it all. She ought to have stayed with the little ones. No one here could give help or even hope. Not fast enough, soon enough, immediately. They all said it was war in England too.

But it wasn't a war as bitter as at home, not as hungry a war. Here, they could fight back because it was an island, and the sea was their friend. And they had the weapons of war.

One of the Englishmen who had been on the ship that dark night out from the Yugoslav coast had brought them all the way here. They had come all the way to this big, old houseful of exiled Poles, kind yet impersonal, busy, sad—all with their own sorrows. They had said that all they could do would be done, but now it was a war, not only for small Pawel in the foothills of the Tatras, but a war all over Europe, in Russia, in North Africa. "We are only Poles, people of a small nation," one woman in uniform had said bitterly. "We must wait until the big ones are ready to help us."

Jan had started some training already. He was to go to Scotland to join the Polish forces there. He wanted to be a pilot, but he had been told he would have to go into the army or the navy depending on what he would best fit into. He

189

should play, play, play music, Wanda thought. He had the gift of giving courage to others.

She could be a nurse in the army or the air force, that they had said. But, she had replied, when the war was over what Poland would need was teachers for the little children. So many of them had been killed by the Nazis. Here, she would have to do what she was told to do.

Everybody was kind. Both of them had been interviewed by many people of their own government in London, and by the English too. But why were they still in London? Why had no one sent help to Pawel?

She rested her forehead against the cold glass of the window and stared into the spring-green park, slowly misting into the evening. Buckingham Palace, with the English King and Queen and their children was still there, despite the air raids. Big Ben would soon toll the hour when Jan would be back to this home-of-many-Poles-away-from-home. Then there would be a dinner she could hardly swallow, remembering the lack at Wit's cottage.

I am not going to cry, she was telling herself when she heard the door open.

There was a long moment's silence.

Then a voice said softly, hopefully, "Wanda? My Wanda?"

The tall man by the door looked even taller because he was so thin, his hair was as blond as

Wanda's and his uniform pocket had a rainbow of ribbons.

"Father? Father!"

They were still sitting there in the dusk when Jan arrived.

He came in with the bitterness and sadness on his face that he and Wanda had shared since their arrival in England.

"Jan," Wanda said, "look, my father has come back."

"Son." Colonel Denin stood up. "Jan. I have many thanks to give you. And much to talk about. But let us have tea as the English do."

He had seen Jan's tears, and he wiped away some of his own as he turned to ring the bell for tea.

Finally, after much talk of Poland, Wanda's father said again; "We are a small country. There is no point in complaining. It does not help at all. We all must do our best, hoping that what we do will help our Poland too. And help will be sent, believe me, for the Allies are not evil, simply they must think of themselves too. They do not understand the Russians as we understand them from centuries of experience, and they do not know about the Germans as we do, also from experience. But they believe, as we believe, in freedom for all freedom-loving peoples. Therefore, we will fight with them and make a brave record of Polish courage, as we have through the centuries."

The evening came through the windows and he went to close the curtains.

"Enough of that, now," he said.

"One more thing, sir," Jan said. "Why have I been kept so long in London when all I wanted to do was to be trained to fly, to fight, to kill the Germans, and fly food out to our own people?"

"You are young, Jan," Wanda's father said. "You will have your share of fighting before the war is over. But also the people here knew I was reporting back to London, and they knew the best medal I could possibly have was to see you two children of my own land. Also, there has been a broadcast organized for Pilsudski Day, the Constitution Day of March seventeenth, and they wanted you to go on the radio, to speak to Poland. They were afraid to talk to you about it because you were only concerned with your own young friends."

"And why not, Father?"

"Because Pawel, and the twins, and the rest of your dear friends are not the only small children who are suffering. I am sorry, sorry."

Colonel Denin turned on the lights in the high old room.

"Think of it. Tonight all our people have been alerted by the underground to listen to a message from London. This message will get through, believe me. And by morning, all the graves, and ruins, and broken statues of our dear heroes will be covered by the red and white flowers of Poland, even if the flowers have been fashioned of paper stolen from the Nazis and tinted red with our blood. Red and white flowers for Poland."

Wanda and Jan stood up. They knew of those flowers. They had helped to make them often.

Wanda's father stood up too. "Go and wash and dress in your best, because we will go soon to speak to Poland. But I have a present for you, a message that came through the underground and was given to me to deliver to you. I think it is news of your friends."

They did not have time to open the envelope and look at the message until they got to the British Broadcasting House, from where the program would go out to Poland. Before they had been able to reach their rooms a messenger had come, and a number of cars had taken them, with many others, through the darkened streets.

Wanda's father and other adults of importance were to go on the air first. Here, in the strange bare room, they stood together as in a desert, left for a moment alone.

Wanda opened the envelope.

"Jan. Look. Surely this must be from Dr. Jerzy because it says all of us are well and Marja sends you new words for the 'Polonaise.' I suppose there was no more time to say anything more. Look, Jan."

"I cannot, cannot play well enough," Jan said, "to say all I want them to know."

193

"But you must try." Wanda took his hand. "For them."

"I'll try."

The official part of the program was finished. The Polish announcer waved Jan and Wanda closer to the microphone while he was still talking, organizing, speaking across miles of space to occupied Poland.

As Wanda sat waiting for someone to tell her what to do, she thought of the square in Warsaw and how there would be thousands of people out. The underground would have sent their secret message that something special was going to happen, something the Nazis didn't expect would come through their loudspeakers. The underground had done it before. And, Wanda thought, Marja and Pawel, Stas, Kazio, Jadwi, Ludwi, Stefan, Zosia, and Dr. Jerzy would probably be somewhere outdoors in Krakow listening too, or perhaps they would be turning on Dr. Jerzy's own secret radio. There would be first of all the guttural voices of the Germans saying the Polish Constitution would never exist again and Pilsudski, the hero, was dead, and threatening and screaming for Poles to obey and be serfs. Then, suddenly their shouting would be cut as she had heard it cut before and the voice of the Polish announcer would ring out.

The small group of Poles in that bare broadcasting room in faraway London sang their National Anthem to their people at home who were forbidden to sing it. The English air trembled with:

"Poland is not yet lost
While still we live . . ."

Out over the Nazi-patrolled streets of Polish towns and villages in the plains and the mountains and in the many hideouts with secret radios, the song rang out, firm and clear.

Then it was time for Jan and Wanda.

As Jan went to the piano he turned and looked at Wanda and nodded. She held firmly in her hands the words written by Marja and sent across the miles by courageous messengers, through danger and fear.

Jan played the first chords. Then he started again, and now she sang to the music, knowing that this was a song not only for their own friends, but for all the children of Poland who whistled and hummed the "Polonaise" to keep up their courage as they went about their dangerous duties, and to Karel, and Jiri, and their friends in Czechoslovakia, and to Tibor and Poldi and the old ladies in Hungary, and to Marko and Trinka and all the others in Yugoslavia who just might be listening at their hidden radio station high in the mountain monastery.

"Day will come when Poland will be free again,
Day will come when war has left the sky and plain,
Day will come when we will have our homes again,
And children will laugh and play
in peaceful meadows of Poland.

"All the world, good friends will be
and people will sing and work together,

In harmony and trust
        for all
And peace
        for all
And love
        for all
And we will be back with our loved ones again
        when the DAY WILL COME. . . ."

The serious new words of Marja's song faded before Wanda's tear-filled eyes. But she sang on with the old words that had once made Jan so angry in the park in Warsaw.

As she sang, another voice joined in, Jan's, singing with her;

"Day will come when we will wash with soap again,
Day will come when we will eat enough again,
Day will come when we will have new shoes again,
        And children will laugh and play
                in peaceful meadows of Poland!"

Epilogue

Most of this story was first written during the Second World War when the events recorded were actually happening. I was working at the time for the *Toronto Evening Telegram* as a reporter, and I also wrote a column called "Darkest Europe" about what was happening in the occupied countries.

Free Polish, Czech, Yugoslav, Norwegian, and Dutch forces were training in Canada and I interviewed literally hundreds of young men and old men, students and politicians, laborers and diplomats, who had contrived to escape from occupied

Europe, hoping to serve their countries with the armies of the Allies.

There came to my desk information from neutral sources; from the Allied Intelligence Services; as well as, for example, from Victor Podolski, the Consul General of Poland in Ottawa. He would send out the releases of the Polish Government in Exile, established in London, such as the *White Book* which was a resume of the activities and achievements of the fighting Poles, both in the underground at home, and abroad. The *Black Book* was a documented report of the atrocities committed by the occupying German forces in Poland. All these documents had been confirmed by neutral observers, sometimes at great personal risk. Since the end of the Second World War, it has become evident that there had been no exaggeration about the atrocities and inhumanity reported by eyewitnesses during the war.

To me, of course, the most heartbreaking were interviews with youngsters like Jan and Wanda, at that time barely younger than myself. I couldn't finish the story well, it was too close. Since then I have visited the scenes of their dangerous days. One early morning, standing outside a climbers' hut high in the Tatra Mountains, I thought of the valiant many who never did get home, and I thought it was time to write their story again.

They believed there would be peace one day. All over the world.

Eva-Lis Wuorio was born in Viipuri, Finland, a Hanseatic seaport. She grew up in Canada where she went to school, became a newspaper columnist, and later a magazine editor. Miss Wuorio, whose books have been published in half a dozen languages, began her writing career as a journalist, covering all sorts of news, from earthquakes and wars to royal weddings. She has worked as a free-lance correspondent in Europe and North Africa and has done a great deal of traveling. From her wide-ranging experiences have come the backgrounds for all her books. *Save Alice!*, a mystery for young readers, was based on her firsthand knowledge of Spain and Ibiza, where she once made her home. The time she spent in Poland just before World War II sets the mood and provides the facts for *Code: Polonaise*. Miss Wuorio now lives on the British Channel Island of Jersey.